Snapshots From My Uneventful Life

Snapshots From My Uneventful Life

David I. Aboulafia

Winchester, UK
Washington, USA

First published by Library Tales Publishing
This Edition published by Roundfire Books, 2018
Roundfire Books is an imprint of John Hunt Publishing Ltd., No. 3 East St., Alresford,
Hampshire SO24 9EE, UK
office1@jhpbooks.net
www.johnhuntpublishing.com
www.roundfire-books.com

For distributor details and how to order please visit the 'Ordering' section on our website.

ISBN: 978 1 78099 292 1
978 1 78099 331 7 (ebook)
Library of Congress Control Number: 2016945824

A CIP catalogue record for this book is available from the British Library.

Design: Stuart Davies

Printed and bound by CPI Group (UK) Ltd, Croydon, CR0 4YY, UK

We operate a distinctive and ethical publishing philosophy in all
areas of our business, from our global network of authors to
production and worldwide distribution.

CONTENTS

"I don't want to achieve immortality through my work…
I want to achieve it through not dying."

Woody Allen

Introduction

THIS BOOK IS DIFFERENT. It will not read like a novel, or even like a group of short stories. It does not have a riveting beginning or a memorable conclusion. It does not portray events chronologically, has no flow to it at all and no discernible order of any kind.

It will never appear on any best sellers list. There will be no made-for-TV movie as a result of its authorship (not even on Lifetime or the Sci-Fi Channel). No critic will marvel at its wondrous prose, or flutter his eyes at its bold and innovative construction.

Hey, *you* could have written this. A thousand-thousand people could have and should have, but they didn't, and that's the point; it was left to me to do it for all of you.

You're welcome.

All things considered, I'm here to tell you that if you're reading this on an airline, having grabbed it impulsively from a shelf fifteen minutes before boarding, then this is really your lucky day. This book is perfect for you. It's not too heavy, and it's going to make you laugh. You'll nod your head wisely and repeatedly in agreement, and say things like "something like that happened to Uncle Henry!" Now and then, it's going to make you think. Most importantly, you can finish it before you de-plane.

I should also tell you that everything you'll read here actually happened. Everything is true. No names have been changed to protect the innocent because no one described here is innocent, especially me. I'm guilty of doing every stupid thing I describe.

So, this is a book of memories. And we all have them, no matter how much beer we drank in college. Perhaps all we really are is a collection of them. But I don't think memories are exactly what we think they are.

All of us make claim to a million recollections, but most of the things we experience each day just seem to evaporate from our

1

minds, never to return. What we call our memories are really just small bits of time, small fragments taken from the experiences of our waking hours. What we remember are moments – weird, tragic, inconsequential, hysterical and revelatory moments – that represent no more than the barest of outlines of the events we lived through.

Let me illustrate:

When I was about eight years old, I constructed a diorama for a grade school project. Into a cardboard shoe box, I arranged colorful cut-outs of soldiers on a battlefield and carefully decorated the interior with trees made of pencils and green paper, grass made of a green packing material spread loosely along the bottom, and cuttings of real plants meant to be bushes. All were affixed to the box with Elmer's Glue.

It had taken me a long time to make and I was proud of it. But, it was more than a bit delicate, and I wanted it to get to school in one piece. I left my apartment early in the morning the next day. All I had to do was wait for the elevator, leave the building, walk across the street, and I would be at school.

I was a bit clumsy at that age, and I suppose I knew it, but I was determined that the project arrive safely and intact. I gripped the box with both hands and fixed my eyes on it, my senses seeking to detect any vibration that might upset the fragile structure. I walked slowly and carefully to my destination, a trek that should have lasted only two to three minutes.

As I was crossing the street – just yards away from the school and with my eyes still riveted on the box – I neglected to notice a huge pothole in the road. My right foot stepped right into it, and I fell hard. And, right on top of my diorama, which was completely crushed beneath me. I arose, sore all over, with a bloody gash on my right wrist. I picked up the flattened art project as if I were removing a crushed squirrel from a highway, slowly retraced my steps back home and enlisted the assistance of Mom. She succeeded in bandaging my open wound, but failed in her attempt to salvage my project.

The event I've just related lasted perhaps a half-hour from start to finish. I remember it vividly – at least enough to tell it to you in detail – though it occurred almost a half-century ago.

But, if I *really* think about that morning – if I concentrate long enough and hard enough – I realize that what I *really* remember are things more like still images than events, mere splinters of time somehow snatched from the continuum that comprised this episode. The true source of my recollection is nothing more than a small group of happenings, each constituting a few seconds of time, like five, three-second videotapes strung together on a continuous loop: Looking at the completed project with pride. Taking a few steps into the road. Looking at my bloodied hand. My mother trying to fix the diorama. My disappointment when I realized she couldn't.

These are the small groups of still life portraits from which we create the moving pictures in our minds. These are the abstracts of our experiences that we call our memories. These are the snapshots of our lives.

These snapshots are the fabric from which we weave our stories, our anecdotes, and our jokes. These snippets of our experiences are from where we derive our simple wisdom. We share them with each other continuously, flinging them across the airwaves, across the internet, and from across the dinner table. With them, we make others laugh, or cry, or think, or feel. Each of us; any of us.

All of us.

Perhaps it is that most of us consider ourselves just ordinary folk, but none of us truly are. Although many of us may feel our lives are largely uneventful, none of our lives can truly be characterized this way, no matter how mundane and commonplace we may think them to be. While our collective memories are like leaves on a tree – every one like the others – each, in their own way, is also unique. All of our snapshots are the singular product of *us*, our environments, and our inimitable perceptions of the world. But, we all have some very similar ones stored away.

Some of our snapshots are thought-provoking. In the best of them there is great comedy and, sometimes, great wisdom, even though they come from only you and me. The problem is that most of us simply take them with us when we leave this earth. They all disappear when we do – everything we've learned, everything we've laughed at, every mistake we've made that we might prevent someone else from making – unless we somehow succeed in passing them along. By recording my abstracts, as I do here, perhaps the essence of what I truly am is preserved. I think that every one of us should consider doing the same.

I'm talking to you, Mister.

So, with no additional fanfare or explanation, I give them all to you, to do with as you wish. I lay before you, with a tongue in my cheek and a twinkle in my eye, the snapshots from my uneventful life.

Soft-Ball

LIKE EVERY BOY GROWING UP ON THE STREETS OF NEW YORK I played baseball, although that wasn't what the sport was called. When I was a kid, baseball was called either *softball* or *hardball*.

Softball was played with either rubber balls or cowhide-covered balls with cork centers, both of which were bigger than hardballs. Hardballs were also covered with cowhide but, unlike softballs, had rocks the size of your fist at their center.

Ladies and gentlemen, trust me when I tell you that a hardball was truly something to be *afraid* of, and perhaps that's why so many city kids never graduated to high school ball or college ball or the pros. You see, in the suburbs, all the baseball fields were manicured pastures of green. In other words, every bounce was a true one, and balls tended to travel precisely where you might have expected them to go.

In the *Bronx*, however, the baseball fields were almost uniformly rock-strewn and ill-maintained. Once the ball touched the ground, it went wherever it wished to go; or perhaps, wherever an angry God decided it should. That's why most of us stuck to softball; because...well because the ball was *softer*, that's why, and because it traveled slower given its greater mass. Also, you could reasonably expect to survive if you were hit by one. Under most circumstances.

So, for many years I played softball, had a team in the league and pitched for my team. I was a reasonably good pitcher, too, but an unreasonably dim-witted one for reasons that will soon become clear.

It happened at a practice somewhere around 1982 and we were all having a good time. Meaning that the air was fresh and clean, the sun was bright and warm and that I was among good friends. And, of course, we were *drinking beer*, so much, in fact, that I couldn't bear to be parted from my can even while I was on the mound. It stood gallantly beside me there, much like a rosin bag, and I reached for it more frequently than I would have that common baseball accessory.

OK, I was *drunk*. But so was Bob when he came to the plate.

Bob was forty at the time and a former police sergeant. He was also six feet tall, two hundred fifty pounds and our clean-up hitter. His body was basically one huge muscle formed into a square.

We were good friends, you see, and we were happy to see each other. *I* was so happy that I began to taunt Bob from the mound. *He* was so happy he responded quite eagerly, which was actually quite difficult, because he was laughing hysterically and gasping for breath as he spoke.

"You're not going to be able to hit anything, are you, Bob?" I asked.

"I could probably hit something down your throat, Dave," he replied between fits of mirth.

"No, Bob, you couldn't because you can't even *see* me, so I'm going to take a few steps forward to give you a clearer view."

With that remark, I did, and then lobbed the ball lazily over the plate. Bob took a truly herculean swing, twisting his entire body like a cork-screw as the bat made contact with nothing but the sweet summer air, and finally collapsed in a gleeful heap on the dirt of the field.

The entire bench exploded with laughter, my teammates holding each other for support and wiping the tears from their eyes. Bob struggled to his feet using his bat for support.

Boy, is he drunk! I thought to myself, as I stepped a few feet closer to the plate. I was surprised that Bob looked so much *bigger* from this new vantage point, even when he looked as *blurry* as he did. But, hell, I was in the middle of a *performance*, and I was only through the first act.

"OK, Bob, I'm going to throw it a little bit slower this time," I said.

"OK, Dave, I'm goin' to send it right back to you in a second," Bob replied.

I allowed myself a pregnant pause and then lobbed the ball again, responding as I did.

"I don't think you'll be able to do that, Bob." Whether Bob's wild peals of laughter began as I threw the ball or as he swung through it for the second time, I don't recall. But, I clearly remember him swinging again and crumpling to the ground in particularly ignominious fashion. Half the players on the bench fell from their seats in hysterics, rolling in the dirt and holding their stomachs for fear their inner organs would somehow be forced through their skins.

Bob rose, but only to his knees, and once more using the bat as a cane. He stayed there for a few seconds, head downcast. Were it not for the fact that he was clearly trying to catch his breath, it might have looked as if he were praying.

Thinking about it now, perhaps he was. Eventually, he rose and entered the batter's box again.

I took a few more steps towards the plate. I realized I had traversed half the distance from the mound to the plate, but the significance of this eluded me. What did not elude me was how far away my *beer* was now, and that bothered me.

I bent down into a pitching stance with a broad smile upon my face.

"I'm going to do everything I can for you now, Bob," I said. "I'm going to give you a pitch even a little baby girl could hit."

I waited another moment. Then, the words spilled from my mouth as the ball lifted from my fingers and floated high into the air.

"But you won't be able to, Bob," I said.

Believe me when I tell you that my timing and delivery were simply perfect. I realized that the next moment would be one of pure comedy, one for the ages; Bob was going to swing through his third strike and fall to the dirt floor of the field in a writhing, quivering heap of hilarity.

I watched the ball descend to the plate. It was only then that I realized Bob had stopped laughing.

When I think of this next snapshot the same image always comes to mind, like a cartoon in my head: It is the white-gloved hand of God Himself reaching down to me from the heavens. I don't know why.

Now, look again at the title of this essay; I'll wait.

Are you finished? OK.

You see, I was about to learn, on the one hand, that both softballs *and* hardballs tend to travel in just about any direction they wish to go. On the other hand, there are some balls that are really incapable of any locomotion at all, no matter how urgent the need may be to *locomotate out of the friggin' way*.

Need I now tell you in what path the ball traveled as Bob crushed it, or at what light speed it appeared to progress when he did?

No. I don't think I do.

Is it relevant whether the softball struck the "left one" or the "right one"?

No. It is not.

I think we're communicating. I think you get it, I really do.

As I got it. At one million miles an hour. I dropped to my knees, which is always appropriate when one receives a message of disapproval so crystal clear directly from the Almighty.

Any man – and *only* a man – who has been struck in this tender area knows the exquisite pain that results. It is not only the *degree* of agony we experience, but the *nature* of the agony that is astonishing, quite memorable, and impossible to describe to anyone *but* a man.

But any man who *has* been hit *there* also knows that the pain tends to pass in a few seconds. And I waited – quite patiently, I thought, under the circumstances – for this *ballular* tribulation to subside. Except, that it did not.

Think of a vise, my friends. Think of a vise that, once closed, is unable to open.

You see, the wives and girlfriends are laughing now. Their men are holding their heads, squeezing their legs shut and trying to get this terrible image out of their minds.

The rest, as they say, is history. I managed to get home – how, I do not know – with the magnitude of the pain exceeding any scale that Charles Richter could have been able to imagine. I limped into the bathroom and removed my pants. And I saw.

What I saw was a sight that I can never quite purge from my head. On the one side, everything was peachy keen. On the other side was something I had never seen before. Something that I had never read about or heard of before. Something that had only a dim relation to anything found in Gray's Anatomy. Something the size of an orange, but the color of an overripe plum.

I think I require medical attention, I thought to myself.

"Yaah – uhhh – yahhh," I cried aloud.

That the hospital's examining physician was gay, I mention only in passing. Somehow, I think that this, too, was a message of some kind, but to present-day its meaning still escapes me.

He gave me a prescription for painkillers. He told me my condition would probably resolve on its own and instructed me to return for a follow-up in one week.

The agony continued without any abatement whatever for three days. No torture inflicted upon anyone in any horror movie, whether by chain saw, hatchet or hot needle, can describe what I went through in that three-day span, popping my prescribed barbiturates twice as often as I should, and writhing on my bed in my own personal hell.

While the pain subsided after the equivalent of a long weekend, what did not abate was the remarkable size of my vital body part, or its astonishing shade of purple, even one week later when I returned to my doctor.

I dutifully lowered my trousers at the physician's command,

lay back and allowed him to perform his examination. I watched him closely as he worked. I was worried, but not *really* worried. After all, he said my condition would resolve itself, and I was feeling much better. Besides, I had a backup plan just in case anything went wrong.

Well, God gave us guys *two*, didn't he? Perhaps *He* had spent a few eons on a softball field somewhere.

All of a sudden, I saw the doctor shake his head back and forth, which I thought was a curious thing for him to do. Then, he spoke: "This may have to come off." That was what he said.

As you may imagine, I was a bit lost for words. So, instead of trying to compose a snappy come-back line, I lurched up abruptly, grabbed him by his lapels with both hands, and gently reminded him that just a few days ago he had said I would be OK.

All right, so I wasn't so gentle, and he became a bit alarmed at my reaction. He urged me to stay calm. That made me laugh. *However* this ended up, *he* would still be able to walk down the street with his body parts swaying rhythmically back and forth, one in perfect balance with the other. He told me to lie back down, and I did.

Only a minute later, the doctor began to shake his head back and forth again. He repeated his former prognosis, made just moments before.

Do you believe me? Perhaps not. Let me be clear, then. This is the phrase he repeated:

"This may have to come off."

With that, my mind and my body went on automatic. I jumped off the examination table and grabbed him again. With my pants hanging around my ankles, I pushed him hard against the wall, his head making a satisfactory *thump* as it struck sheet rock. I spoke to him through clenched teeth, my face only inches from his, reminding him once again of his original advice.

Rather terrified at this point, he suggested I get a second

opinion. I concurred. So, I went to a "specialist."

I quickly learned that there are no *ball* doctors in New York City. There are, however, plenty of urologists, and, more precisely, urologists who are also surgeons.

The doctor's office was quite impressive, with oak paneling throughout, and a large cherry wood desk that only a skilled physician would possess. He was calm and matter-of-fact. There was no examination, but there was a *consultation*.

He was really quite pleasant. He looked at my medical records, and we had a nice chat. But he was unable to offer a prognosis of any kind. This confused me. After all, there were thousands of softball players in New York, and he surely must have seen this type of unfortunate mishap happen to someone once before.

I asked him why he was unable to form an opinion. His response was quite memorable.

"Well, I can't tell anything until I get *in* there," he said.

"You mean surgery?" I asked.

"Exactly," he replied.

Once again, I of the quick wit and spontaneous one-liner was lost for words. Skilled physician that he was, he recognized my predicament immediately and responded accordingly, his words soft and measured, the confidence fairly brimming from his lips as he spoke.

"Listen," he said. "There's nothing to be concerned about. The worst that will happen is that we'll just remove it and put in a prosthetic."

"A prosthetic?" I queried.

"Yes," he replied.

I considered this carefully for a moment. "You mean like a ping pong ball?" I asked. He thought this rather amusing and chuckled gamely.

"Kind of like that," he said, still chuckling. "Pop it right out, pop it right in. Nothing to it."

"Nothing to it," I repeated. I felt my lower lip drop and brush the plush carpet of his immaculate office. An image of an assault rifle appeared suddenly in my mind. I wasn't sure why.

"Nothing to be alarmed about," he reiterated. "After all, God gave us guys a backup plan, didn't He?"

He smiled broadly. I smiled back just as broadly, shook his hand and thanked him for his time. I said I would consider what he had said and call him the next day. In reality, I wished him a slow, agonizing death, and vowed if I ever saw him again I would terminate him on the spot.

I then decided to see a *real* doctor. A *real doctor* would give me a more acceptable prognosis. In other words, he would not suggest the slicing, dicing, removal or replacement of a part of my anatomy I had really grown quite attached to over the years.

Specifically, I went to see the associate director of urology at Beth Israel Hospital in Manhattan. I lay down on an examination table at his request, and he began his inspection of the goods. He began to shake his head back and forth.

This action did not produce anxiety or angst as you might expect, but it did make me think.

After all, having narrowly avoided the cold-blooded murder of my two prior physicians, I truly wondered whether I possessed the necessary resilience to avoid butchering this one, at least before he decided to do the same to me. As it turned out, no capital crime was required.

"Must've hurt," he stated, undoubtedly with nothing but scholarly and solicitous intent.

Must have, I thought to myself. "Ya' think?" I replied.

"Were you on any pain medication?" he asked. I produced a half-empty vial of painkillers from my pocket. He examined the bottle.

"How long did you take these for?" he asked. "Three days," I replied.

"Good thing," he said.

"Why is that?" I innocently inquired.

"Because, in two more days, you probably would've been dead," he replied.

"Really," I said.

It wasn't a question. After all that had happened, I wasn't capable of being surprised anymore by anything.

"Really," he repeated.

The doctor explained that I had suffered serious internal bleeding. He also explained that the medication I had taken acted as a blood thinner, preventing proper clotting. In other words, unbeknownst to me, I had continued to bleed as long as I was on the medication and would have as long as I continued to take it. Until I was all out, I suppose. Of blood, not pills.

In any event, I confess I have set you up for a happy ending, and I am pleased to note that most of the stories you'll read here end in just this way. No surgery was necessary, and no serious disability worth reporting to you resulted, as the existence of my two daughters happily attests.

There is only one footnote to this tale. You see, I was still quite swollen, and apparently would be for a while. Put another way, I was *huge*. Put yet another way – and forgive me for being so crass, but I really feel I need to make my point, here – you'll need to imagine stuffing an orange into a pair of tight jeans, and then imagine what *that* might look like to an innocent passerby.

As it turned out, imagination was not required. My next snapshot puts me on the streets of Woodside, New York, returning to my apartment. Walking towards me was a rather attractive young woman. When she approached to a distance of about ten feet, she stopped dead in her tracks. She gasped, and focused her gaze upon a place where I assure you there was neither fruit stand nor orange grove anywhere to be seen.

Maybe this isn't so bad, I thought to myself.

The Snake

BETWEEN THE AGES OF EIGHT AND EIGHTEEN, I lived in an apartment in a 20-storey high-rise in the Bronx, NY. It rested on a high rocky hill and had an outlandish yellow brick exterior accented by green terrace dividers that stood out for miles. One side of the apartment building – the side I lived on – looked out over the East Bronx, a relatively unattractive hodgepodge of roads and buildings. The first thing one would notice about the view – sweeping from my eighteenth-story vista – was the elevated trains that ran twenty-four hours a day. It took some doing to learn to sleep with the interminable din of those iron horses ringing in your ears at all hours of the night.

The view from the other side of the building was magnificent. It faced the northeastern most section of the famous Botanical Gardens just a city block away. The outer sliver of this part of the gardens could be accessed by crossing a short, elevated bridge constructed over the Bronx River Parkway. In the winter, some kids would cross that bridge and ride their sleds down the infamous *Snake Hill* located just on the other side. No one could make it down without a crash landing of some kind, and no one would travel further than the confines of the hill itself, because to them nothing else was there. To me, however, this part of the park was the closest thing to a magical forest that I'd ever seen. It was almost completely undeveloped and deserted most of the time. Here, you could find woods and wildlife in what was otherwise a concrete jungle. I spent a lot of time there – usually playing hooky and in a contemplative state – and there's where I found it one day.

It was just a common garter snake, about a foot long, harmless, with blue/green/grayish skin. Still, no wild animals – other than pigeons and rats – are really *common* in New York, so I did what any self-respecting city boy would do; I took it home.

I don't recall asking my mother's permission, and I'm not sure it was required, although she found out about it soon enough. I placed it in a black, five-gallon aquarium, fitted with a hood and a fluorescent light. I placed the tank on the lower level of a wrought iron stand that held a larger 20-gallon tank for tropical fish above. I decorated the small enclosure in such manner as a fine snake would appreciate.

It seemed quite happy in its new home: that is, until it wasn't. I assume this only because one day it simply left.

How it crawled out I was never sure, but it did, and I tore my room apart looking for it. I hoped it hadn't migrated outside of my room, underneath the crack of the door, because if it were found anywhere else – say, in my father's bedroom – its fate (and mine, by logical operation) was truly uncertain.

Anyway, my mother – who came to my room every fifteen minutes to check on the progress of my search – was becoming more agitated as time passed. So was I, and eventually I just collapsed in a heap in the center of my bedroom, which was now strewn with the contents of every drawer, every cabinet, every closet and shelf. There was nowhere I hadn't looked. It wasn't there.

Except that it was. Frustrated and exhausted, from my vantage point on the floor I looked up to the five-gallon tank and its secure lid, and then, to the sturdy, wrought iron stand that held the tank aloft. I noticed the snake curled around one of its decorative trestles; looking at me intently and appearing quite amused, at least, by *snakey* standards.

It took me ten seconds to place the beast back in its glass cage and two hours to clean up my room, talking to it all the while, telling it it would never escape again, that it was a lifer, and that it was lucky escaping prisoners weren't shot in the Bronx.

I was a determined teenager. When my room was reasonably clean, and with the snake looking thoroughly satisfied with itself, I took a brick being used as a bookend and simply used it as a brick, placing it on the top of the light fixture in the center of the tank's cover. I checked around the edges of the tank to make sure there was a tight seal. Satisfied, I stood up, hands on my hips.

"Try getting out of that!" I challenged.

I lay down on my bed and took a two-hour nap. And, when I awoke, the snake was gone.

I closed my eyes, thinking I was still dreaming. I opened my eyes and looked again. The snake was still gone.

I had heard of Sherlock Holmes, of course, but I had never read any of Sir Arthur Conan Doyle's novels about the inscrutable English detective. This was unnecessary, as I had watched several Sherlock Holmes movies starring the great actor Basil Rathbone. And I was fully aware of the celebrated sleuth's most famous maxim: that when you have eliminated the impossible, whatever remains, however improbable, must be the truth.

I inspected the tank again. Although it was chock full of rocks and fake plants and other snake toys, there was no place for it to hide. There had been no way for it to get out. So, I deduced in Holmesian fashion that, however unlikely it might seem, the snake was still there; there – right in front of my eyes – but, somehow *not* there.

I removed the brick and placed it aside. I removed the fluorescent fixture, holding it in my right hand, and with my left removed the tank's cover and placed that aside. I looked in the tank.

Empty. I ran my hand inside the tank. Nothing.

It was there, nevertheless. Inspired by nothing less than an angel or similarly divine entity, I looked at the light fixture in my hand. And, I remembered.

Snakes are cold-blooded animals. They seek the light, and heat. I turned the fixture upside down, bulb side up. My pet had worked itself behind the fluorescent bulb of the fixture, seeking the meager warmth it provided and, undoubtedly, having another huge laugh at my expense.

The next day, I brought the snake back to its home and watched it crawl its way back into the grass in that unlikely urban forest. I lost a pet that day but gained three small bits of wisdom: That one should be hesitant to remove an animal from its natural surroundings; that Sir Doyle was quite the genius; and, that snakes really do have a sense of humor.

Horror Dogs

I HAVE ALWAYS HAD A PENCHANT FOR HORROR MOVIES. From the earliest days of *The Twilight Zone* and *The Outer Limits* I've sought out the genre. The black and white varieties commanded my attention at first; the immortal classics of Frankenstein, the Wolfman, Dracula and the Mummy. These gave way to the movies of Peter Cushing and Christopher Lee in their hundreds of incarnations and reincarnations as vampires, monsters, and monster-vampire hunters. From there, I graduated to every conceivable horror flick regardless of quality.

In my mid-twenties, I had a job for the world famous Joseph Bulova School, a vocational rehabilitation facility located in the town of Woodside, in the Borough of Queens. There, I found myself blessed by my first great boss, whose unique management style included letting me do whatever I wished.

That included leaving work at 4:55 each afternoon, giving me just enough time to run home and catch the remarkable *Chiller Theatre* and its collection of old horror films which commenced at 5 o'clock. I was able to accomplish this because I lived in a two-family house right next door, given to me *gratis* in exchange for my duties as the 24-hour supervisor of the school's dormitory.

As I began my regular sprint home one day, I realized that I lacked a necessary and critical tool that was an essential element of my television viewing: Devil Dogs.

For those uninitiated, Devil Dogs are torpedo shaped chocolate cakes (actually shaped like the "photon torpedoes" in *Star Trek*) with a cream or marshmallow center. What collection of chemicals, preservatives, artificial sweeteners, colors or other man-made inventions and additions to the periodic table are contained within these tempting sweets I do not know. At that age, I truly didn't care. They were, and remain to this day, an absolutely delicious treat.

Devil Dogs are as addictive as any illegal drug. However, while drugs might have rewarded me with a similarly stimulating high, the possession of same might have been accompanied by a most unwelcome detention by the authorities. This would have obviated the entire purpose of the indulgence. Namely, to enhance the *Chiller Theatre* experience.

Still, it was five minutes to show time, and I was, as they say, *Devil Dogless*. Always a man of quick decision and command, I leaped into my car – which in those days was a black 1968 Camaro that looked a lot faster than it really was – and headed for the nearest bodega, just a few blocks away. This required racing down narrow side streets at about sixty miles an hour, but hey; this was *Devil Dogs and Chiller Theatre we were talking about here!*

With rising blood pressure and an increasing awareness that time was short, I skidded to a stop in front of the corner store, lucky to find an empty spot right there. I thrust the car door open, narrowly missed being sideswiped by a passing bus and scooted inside, paying no attention to the annoying ring of the chimes placed just above the entrance door which heralded my arrival.

My eyes widened at the sight of the very first food item they saw: Devil Dogs, stacked three boxes deep and three boxes high, and right at my eye level on a shelf opposite the store's front door. "God will provide," I whispered to myself, genuinely grateful for the existence of a higher power. Having made my purchase, and clutching the white box of *Doggies* to my chest, I drove home and burst into my apartment leaving my key in the front door. I fairly leaped towards the television, my hand wildly seeking the *on* switch. As I waited for the box to warm up, I tossed the Devil Dogs on a small cocktail table containing a phone and a lamp, situated to the left of the couch, facing the television. I raced to the front door, removed my key, closed the door and rapidly pulled down all the curtains in the room making it as dark as possible.

I settled in. I had missed the opening credits of the show – where old monsters from the '30s, '40s and '50s parade across the screen in a brisk and ghastly procession – but the main feature was just beginning.

Which was "Them." Oh, this was too much. *THEM.* Giant ants – the unforeseen product of atomic testing – attack a bunch of teenagers and battle the United States Army.

I MEAN FRIGGIN' GIANT ANTS, MAN! I reached for the Devil Dogs and proceeded to dine, my eyes glued to the screen. There was no need for light; my hand was steady and practiced, and in mechanical fashion I consumed one after the other, after the other, as teenage girls wailed, teenage boys in leather jackets tried to look brave, and gigantic mutated insects pitted their black, claw-like mandibles against our courageous servicemen.

Somewhere in the middle of the movie the phone rang. I ignored it. It rang again; I ignored it again. On the fourth ring, I cursed to myself, remembering who I had foolishly told to call me just at that time. I turned on the light, picked up the phone and began my conversation. This would be quick.

As I spoke, my eyes drifted to the half-eaten box of twelve Devil Dogs on the cocktail table. Something struck my eye. I abruptly ended my call, but I continued to stare at the box. A strange thought entered my mind.

"It's not St. Patrick's Day," I mused to myself. I had a second thought, and I spoke it aloud. "It's not even March; St. Patrick's Day is in March."

Then, I had a third thought, one which naturally followed the first two. "Devil Dogs are not green."

OK. I believe I had established that those chocolaty Devil Dogs with the white cream filling were not green. Since it wasn't St. Patrick's Day, I couldn't expect this box to represent a special holiday promotion by those fine people at Drakes. I picked up the box and peered inside for a closer inspection, thinking my eyes had deceived me.

Every one of the six remaining Devil Dogs was green. I didn't have to be a lawyer to conclude, *ipso facto*, that the six I had already consumed had been green as well, the unmistakable result of that unpleasant and often gastronomically disturbing fungus known as *mold*.

I didn't get sick from the episode, but I didn't eat any Devil Dogs for the two following decades either, substituting in their place the always popular Hostess Cup Cakes, which I continue to enjoy to this day. Typically, in well-lit rooms, and equipped with my eyeglasses.

How To Almost Get Rid Of Your Wife On Your Honeymoon

I SHOULD HAVE KNOWN it was going to be an unusual honeymoon when the beautiful hotel my beautiful wife and I arrived at in Barbados, just 24 hours after taking our vows, could not locate our reservation, despite the fact that it had been booked and paid for three months in advance.

We arrived at our destination with my wife, still the blushing bride, ogling over the fantastical and beautiful and lush surroundings. I approached the counter to attend to the business of checking in. A truly lovely woman there began to struggle mightily with her undoubtedly advanced computer, a small bead of sweat forming on her furrowed brow, as my wife spun round and round the lobby oohing and aahing like Cinderella after the ball.

Wifey didn't get it yet. But I got it right away. The desk clerk smiled sweetly.

"Just have a seat; I'll get the manager for you," she said.

My wife overheard this remark, I'm sure, but certainly had every reason to believe that the hotel staff knew we had just tied our nuptial knot. The manager simply wished to greet us personally; that was all.

HAH! Fat chance.

The manager soon appeared, sporting a Caribbean accent, an Italian suit and a French manicure. Ever so politely, he asked us to sit down in the lobby and "can I get you a drink?"

So impressed was my wife by this nurturing posture that she happily agreed to a drink and so what if she hadn't had lunch and we were still hung over from the night before?

I, of course, knew better. *I* knew that he was buttering us up for something and that an atomic bomb of some kind was about to drop on our honeymoon plans. But, *I* certainly didn't want *him* to know that I knew.

"Drink? Sure!" I replied enthusiastically, a broad smile brightening my countenance.

The refreshments arrived, and my wife gulped greedily, remarking to the man – who she was already *so* impressed with – how absolutely *stunning* everything was. He smiled demurely. I pretended to take a sip from my drink and kept a smile on my face, watching the manager intently.

He smiled again. He blushed. He introduced himself. He said he was flattered. He welcomed us. He added these words: "We have a little problem..."

His smile disappeared. Now he just looked vexed and concerned, as if he had inadvertently trod on a puppy dog's tail.

"Problem?" I innocently inquired.

I already knew there was a "problem." Now, I was just going to find out what it was. But I could guess.

"We've overbooked, and we have no rooms available," he announced rather succinctly.

I decided to drink my drink after all, but the manager continued speaking. My wife, however, heard only his last remark, after which she became quite deaf. Her world began to slip away from her into parts unknown.

Suffice it to say that hurricanes do occur in Barbados, but that volcanoes do not, so I knew that the hapless manager could not have been prepared for the eruption that spewed forth from my beloved. As she screamed and cried and raged, I kept calm and kept looking at the administrator, only because it was obvious to me that he still had something of substance to say. I held my wife's hand and cooed gentle assurances into her ear. I encouraged the shaken man to proceed.

"We do have a sister hotel," he continued apologetically, wiping the sweat from his brow with a silk handkerchief, "and it's right down the road. We can put you there for a few days and then move you right back here." He brightened instantly at the brilliance of his suggestion.

We had no choice, of course, so the staff packed our bags into a white golf cart and we were escorted to what appeared to be a staircase leading to the back entrance of an apartment building. It did not look promising – in fact, it looked like the beginning of a kidnapping or a drug transaction – but we gamely proceeded on.

At the top of a rickety staircase was a nondescript door, and I almost closed my eyes as I entered, mumbling to myself, "This can't be good." It wasn't.

It was remarkable. What greeted us was a $3,000 a night, three-bedroom, two-floor luxury condo on the beach. It had a huge living room surrounded by hundreds of feet of glass and terrace and it was magnificent. As we entered, we noticed a register located on a small table. This, apparently, was a famous room previously inhabited by famous people and all were required to make their mark in this book, which we did.

There was a bit of trouble getting us *out* of that room, but that's another story I shall not go into. Nevertheless, the first day of our honeymoon is part of family lore; this is what you're supposed to be suffering through, and this is what you bought into. So just sit back and suck it up.

Anyway, this was just the opening act preceding my wife's brush with death and my heroic actions to save her, events typically described only in comic books and graphic novels filled with amazing superheroes. This is what happened…

We were taking a bus ride, hours into the mountains, where there was this amazing site we just *had* to see. Typically, I reject everything and anything *turista* while on vacation and tours by bus are *definitely turista*, so I usually prefer to see the local sights from behind the wheel of my rented car. I reserve to myself the singular pleasure of narrowly avoiding wild goats on four-foot wide dirt roads, on death-defying mountain passes in *who knows where*.

But, this was our honeymoon, you see, and I wanted my wife

to have all of my attention. So we took off together, me, as the dutiful and adoring husband, holding her hand and gazing lovingly into her eyes the entire ride.

At least, that's how I remember it.

Anyway, we reached the top of the mountain. We separated from the group and walked into a beautiful, grass-filled meadow. The pasture trailed steeply down the mountaintop for about a hundred feet and ended with a large stand of pine trees. Three feet beyond the border of pines was a precipice and what appeared to be about a 2,500-foot clear drop from there. There was no fence or guardrail of any kind. The phrase *lover's leap* comes to mind.

The view of the surrounding mountains and, beyond that, of the island itself, was truly beautiful. Being a photographer as well as a writer – and, of course, being a man in love on his honeymoon – I couldn't resist capturing the image of my lovely, glowing bride amid that natural splendor. I remained at the top of the meadow. I encouraged Andrea to walk down to a spot a few yards before the trees so I could immortalize this grand moment for all time.

She did. She turned to pose. She smiled. But I had overlooked something.

It had rained the night before, and hard. The tall grass of the lovely meadow before us craftily concealed a thick layer of mud from the overnight storm, which we discovered when my wife's feet slipped from underneath her and she began to slide.

Andrea is rarely demure, has little difficulty expressing herself clearly when she wishes to and did so on this occasion. She began to scream, and quite loudly, her shrieks accompanied by that magic word heard so often in the annals of *comic book-dom*: *"Help!"*

This was the moment of my finest hour. This was a moment when a man was called upon to be something more than a man. When destiny whispered in his ear and told him it was his turn.

Perhaps a lesser man, looking on from that mean and hopeless distance, would have wrung his hands and whimpered, *"Andrea – Oh Andrea!"* as his wife slid off the mountaintop to a dreadful and somewhat untidy demise. Perhaps a quick-thinking and decisive man would have immediately turned to summon help, or looked for a rope, or the Barbados Fire Department, or a rescue dog, or a long vine, or…

No. This was a time for action. This was a time for heroes. There wasn't much time to muse as Andrea continued her vociferous slide towards the trees and, beyond that narrow stand, toward the thin border separating her from nothing but the clear mountain air.

So, I did what I did. I tossed my camera away and began a mad dash down the hill, knowing as I did that I would never be able to stop. I guessed I would worry about that if I got to my wife before she flew right off the mountain.

As I ran – picking up speed and somehow managing to stay on my feet – the outline of a plan formed in my mind. This was more difficult than it sounds because Andrea's wild screeches were quite distracting.

Nonetheless, I thought that my only chance at rescue was to slide just before I reached her, as if I were sliding into second base during a softball game. Then, just before she arrived at the edge, I would grab a pine with my left hand and snag her with my right, saving my wife, and her life, and the day, and everything else that came along with it. What would undoubtedly follow from this happy result would be a public ceremony and an award from the prime minister of the island.

Or perhaps, a one-way ticket back home along with a fond and hearty *good riddance* from that head of state.

Well, it was a plan, anyway; hastily formed by the time I was halfway down. After another moment or so, I was the *second* halfway down, so I had no option but to implement it. Just as Andrea's squealing, shrieking, squawking form passed through the trees towards the cliff's edge I began my slide. I grabbed a large sapling with my left hand and extending my body as far as it would extend, I grabbed her by the arm. Miraculously, I hung on to both tree and wife and lay there, stretched like a rubber band.

Now, *I* screamed, as every muscle I owned in both of my arms snapped from the effort. But, Andrea's slide had ceased, and I relaxed my hold.

We both got up slowly and carefully, and held on to each other for fear we would slip again. We were covered in mud from head to toe. But before we turned to begin our slow and cautious ascent up the mount, I gently took my wife's hand and led her back in the direction she had been heading just moments before.

I needed to see. I needed to look into the abyss. I had to see what my singular heroism had saved her from.

We walked through the trees, to the slim border of grass just beyond and then peered over the edge of the drop. And we saw.

What had looked from my earlier vantage point as a fall from which certain death would result was, in fact, a mild depression of two feet followed by a broad, grass-filled plateau which would have assured a landing both safe and soft.

A part of me was mildly disappointed, I admit, and I was grateful I did not need to remind my wife that it is the thought that should count in such situations.

We returned to the bus and sat miserably on the red plastic-covered seats with heads downcast, holding hands. Our fellow sightseers returned one by one. Each and every one glared at us with disapproving eyes and sneered and chortled at our appearance for the entire ride back to the hotel, as if we had rudely hijacked this idyllic experience from them by frolicking wildly in muck and mire, as unrestrained American newlyweds are clearly wont to do.

Boy

HE WAS A MEDIUM-SIZED DOG, not possessing the size or strength typically found in the German Shepherd breed, but his markings and his spirit were all shepherd. My father found him on the streets of the Bronx. He called, "Come here, boy." He came, and he stayed, and the name stuck. The dog became a family legend.

When I was a small child, he patiently allowed me to climb onto his back and pull his ears. I ate his dog biscuits and he ate the cookies given to me by my parents to help reduce the pangs of teething. He would be "walked" by opening the door to our third-story apartment and allowing him to trot down the stairs himself. He would then wait for someone to open the lobby door, take his jaunt, and simply reverse the process when he wished to return.

These days, few city-dwellers would do this with any dog. I suppose everyone thought it was OK, back then, at least with this dog. The neighborhood knew him, I guess, and he knew the neighborhood and could take care of himself. Among the many stories told about Boy are these...

My parents originally lived on Bainbridge Avenue, several miles from where they would reside between the time of my fourth and eight birthdays on Valentine Avenue. Boy had made himself a canine friend on Bainbridge; a small mutt that would pass the day away looking out of a ground floor window.

One day, after we moved, during one of his routine "walks," Boy failed to return. By the third day of his absence, my parents panicked and finally jumped into the car to search for him. On a hunch, they took the fifteen-minute drive back to their old neighborhood. They found Boy lying beside that ground floor window, waiting patiently for his small companion to return.

"He was visiting," my mother explained.

My parents took him everywhere they went. In the '50s, they drove across this great country with Boy along for the entire ride. They stopped somewhere in the Midwest – at a small restaurant, for provisions – and then started their quest again. About an hour later, they looked in the back seat and discovered Boy was gone.

They drove fifty miles back to the pit stop they had last frequented in the hope that he had simply jumped out there. Upon arriving, they were greeted by the sight of a crowd of people who had formed a circle in front of the diner. In the center of the circle was Boy.

He was never a particularly aggressive or fearsome dog, despite his ancestry, and his sweet face, smallish-size and natural good looks usually made him appear the charmer. But not that day. He sat in the center of the circle growling fiercely, baring his teeth and holding the crowd at bay, not allowing anyone to approach him.

No one appeared particularly scared. They were just trying to win him over – unsuccessfully – with offers of food and water. He simply refused to be touched until his owners returned for him. But perhaps the most amazing tale about Boy occurred during my parent's flight from New York City to Los Angeles, also during the '50s. In those days, all animals were considered mere freight and were shipped to their various destinations in separate cargo planes located at a separate terminal on the far side of the airport. Boy was placed in a wooden enclosure designed by my father – who had a woodworker's patience and skill – and delivered to the terminal for transport. My parents then got in their car, drove to the opposite end of the massive, crowded airport, parked the vehicle, walked to the terminal and waited on line to consign their luggage. Until my father looked down and saw the bloody and battered sight of his faithful dog beside him.

Boy had destroyed his crate in record time and at great cost to his physical self. He then managed an improbable escape from the terminal. He followed the scent of my parents for well over a mile, circumvented twisting roads and ramp ways, dodged scores of vehicles and people, and traversed through who-knows-how-many closed doors. He arrived – impossibly, miraculously – at my father's feet prior to boarding.

As I write, I realize that Boy has been dead for over fifty years. His life is only a dim memory. In fact, I have only a single snapshot of him, taken when I was four years old. It's an image of me asking my father why Boy would no longer come when called.

"He's an old dog, now," my father explained.

To this day, the still photos and ancient moving pictures that memorialize his brief life still evoke a smile, and a sad sigh.

A Funny Gag, But No Laughing Matter

POOR COCO, my one-year-old, chocolate brown, 65 pound, positively loony Standard Poodle, was about to get his balls chopped off.

Look, there's just no delicate way to describe it, and I'm not sure whether I should tiptoe around anything or sugar coat the true nature of the event. Employing a more acceptable term such as "neuter" would not alter the graphic significance of such a procedure, at least to any human male.

While convinced of the necessity for this long ago, and despite the sage assurances of the capable veterinarians we consulted (who, I assure you, would just as quickly have recommended the de-balling of my canary or koala), I could not shake the disturbing notion that my loving pet's very *soul* would be affected in some way.

Maybe he would come out of surgery like a Stepford wife, or like one of those pod-people who are just like the humans they replace, except that they're not.

That bothered me. That, and the fact I couldn't even discuss the issue with the vet without two hands shielding my gonads. Hey, don't wave a red flag in front of a bull, if you know what I mean.

Anyway, my wife took him to the vet that day. Before Coco left, I approached him with bowed head as if he were going to the gallows. I said I was sorry I'd failed him, that I'd done everything I could, but, that it would be over quickly and he wouldn't feel a thing.

French Poodles are among the smartest dogs on the planet and Coco is no exception. He's also a *crap* expert, as most dogs tend to be, and is fully able to recognize it when it's exiting the mouth of his human. He looked at me with disdain and disbelief, snarling at my disingenuousness, and I didn't blame him a bit.

The task of retrieving my pup, several hours later, fell to me. This is a duty that has always caused me great pain and anguish. How it is possible for a man to get as anxious over the health of his dog as the health of his children I can't understand, but I do. I drove to the vet with feelings of dark anticipation and dread.

My anxiety expresses itself through my comedy, I suppose, or in the attempt, at least. I guess it's a way of expelling bad thoughts. I entered the clinic and approached the five sweet but always distracted female administrators who crowded the small area that was the front office. Separating them from the patient waiting area was a four-foot high barrier, which they no doubt thought steep enough to fend off any large beast weighing more than any of those sheltered behind it.

"I'm here to pick up Coco," I announced stoutly. "I *believe* that he was spayed," I added.

On the one hand, I was quite proud of my use of complex medical terminology. On the other hand, I didn't mind disclaiming a precise awareness of the procedure, so I'd at least have culpable deniability if anyone were to think me cruel or unfeeling for having so mercilessly mutilated my pet.

"You mean *neutered*, I hope," pleaded one of the oh-so-kind assistants, reminding me that the term "spay" is most often used in connection with the female of the species. She spoke with a curious narrowing of her left eye as if to assess whether I might have brought the animal in for a sex change.

"Oh, yes, I'm sorry," I cheerfully agreed. Wishing to clarify the matter, I simply added that Coco had been brought in to get his balls chopped off, and that was the long and the short of it.

As you can imagine, this remark was received with some disapproval.

Then, I got an idea. I giggled to myself. I forced myself serious and looked around to see if anyone was in earshot of my thoughts. Finding no one – and somewhat disappointed – I leaned forward.

"May I ask you something?" I inquired of the wholly efficient two-kids-three-cats-mom assistant in front of me.

"Of course," she replied.

"Can I keep them?" I asked. Everyone in the office area stopped what they were doing and looked up.

"Excuse me?" she asked.

Timing was everything and I knew it. I floated a pregnant pause and repeated, "Can I keep them?"

"You want to keep them?" she asked.

"Yes...well, actually, it's my wife who wants them."

"Your wife?"

Everyone was at full attention now and I'd achieved what I'd set out to: namely, to make a complete spectacle of myself.

"Yes," I replied. "She wants to keep them in a jar on the mantle."

"In a jar?" she asked with some astonishment.

"Yes," I repeated.

"On the mantle?" she asked.

"Yes..." I replied, quite eagerly now. I was ready for my close-up, baby; ready to deliver the punch line.

"She wants to display them right next to mine," I added happily.

Well, *I* thought it was funny. Most of my audience laughed, getting the gag.

But, in relief, I'm sure.

Asleep At The Wheel

THERE ARE PEOPLE WHO MERELY SLEEP, and then there are people who seem to pass out, disappear altogether, and locate themselves to another dimension.

I think everyone knows someone like this. I met my first such character when I was thirteen, at the Swan Lake sleep-away camp in upstate New York. "Big Jim" was a camp counselor, soft-spoken and unassuming; with black rimmed eyeglasses that he never removed even when he was sleeping. He was also six-foot-four, heavily muscled and physically imposing. He didn't talk very much and everyone viewed him as a good guy. But his ability to enter into a death-like slumber was legendary and tested early one Sunday morning.

For one reason or another, a half dozen of us awoke from the bunkhouse next to Big Jim's just after sunrise, with the same idea in our heads. I don't really know how this is possible, but I suppose that mischief and girls are the two common themes circulating in the brains of all thirteen-year-old boys.

We rushed into our clothing. With little discussion, and as if of one mind, we tiptoed out of the bunkhouse to the grass outside. One kid produced a cherry bomb. He appeared to have slept with it hidden in his pajamas.

As you may know, a cherry bomb is a red ball about the size of your thumb. Inside is black powder and it's equipped with a green fuse that, once lit, will burn under dirt or underwater or under anything for that matter.

A cherry bomb is not a mere firecracker. It is distinguishable not only by its size and the boom it produces, but by the number of digits it can remove from your hand if it's defective or misused.

Thirteen-year-olds are not deterred by such hypothetical concerns; so another kid produced a book of matches.

We looked at each other. We looked at the bunk where Big Jim and his innocent charges slept. We looked at each other again and at the bunkhouse again. We all knew what we were going to do, and we all knew there were two ways we could carry it out.

Option one: One kid opens the door: a second holds the bomb: a third kid lights it and the second one throws it inside. Everyone runs like crazy.

Option two: Some brave soul quietly slips inside, lights the explosive and throws it under Big Jim's bed. Everyone runs like crazy, especially the brave soul.

Option one was safe and effective – for us, at least – but we all agreed it was a little too easy. Hell, *anyone* could blow something or someone up like that. We needed to get this under Big Jim's bed. We needed to see whether it would wake him up and whether the legends were true. However, option number two required not only that someone sneak in undetected, but exit undetected as well, past a bunkhouse full of slumbering teenagers, and in lightning fashion once the fuse was lit. For some reason, everyone looked at me. Feeling an obligation to advance something, I suggested a third option.

We would take a cigarette and put it at the end of the fuse. Someone would sneak in, put the bomb under Big Jim's bed, and light the cigarette. When it burned down it would ignite the fuse. The difficulty of entering and exiting undetected remained, but this option provided time within which to make a potentially safe retreat. We decided on option three.

None of us saw the need to discuss the negligible statistical possibility that the *someone* igniting the thing might be blown up along with everyone else inside.

All eyes remained on me, which, in the years that followed, became a common occurrence in such circumstances. Anytime someone planned to do something completely stupid they usually found me willing to assist, if not lead the effort altogether. Practically speaking, I was small, I was quick, and I was stealthy when I was not being clumsy, and if no teenage girls appeared, I thought I could pull it off.

One kid rummaged through his pocket and produced a cigarette broken neatly in two. I took one half from his sweaty palm. From the second boy, I took the book of matches. I opened it sagely and inspected its contents. I took the cherry bomb from the third and carefully inserted the half-cigarette over the fuse. It looked good; it really did. One of the kids advanced to the screen door and opened it for me, a gesture of respect and consideration I really did appreciate. The door opened noiselessly, as did the heavier, unlocked door beyond it. I entered.

Big Jim's twin bed was about fifteen feet to my left. He filled all of it and more and his feet dangled at least a foot off its end. I tiptoed over and sneaked a terrified glance at the several other kids I had to pass – like a gauntlet – along the way. All were in slumberland. Big Jim's black-rimmed glasses were still on his head, as expected. His head was tilted back; his mouth open cavernously, and every few seconds a deep rumbling snore would erupt from his lips. Apparently, all the other occupants had gotten used to this long ago.

I knelt at Big Jim's bedside, struck a match, and lit the cigarette. I watched it as it burned, my anxiety rising with the smoke, but I knew there was one inch between the glow at the end of the butt and the fuse inserted within it. I placed it under his bed gingerly and quietly snuck out.

We all ran back to our bunks, each of us pulling our covers tightly around our necks. We giggled in anticipation and waited. A full minute went by; a minute that seemed to last a year.

The explosion that ensued was truly memorable, and the small confines of the bunkhouse amplified the result considerably. At the boom we lurched from our beds and dashed outside. Huge clouds of white smoke poured from the door as kids stumbled out in a daze. We watched, exhausted from the effort required to play dumb and amazed at the effectiveness of our handiwork. One by one, all inside staggered out safely. All except one.

I was the first to re-enter the bunkhouse. It stank of sulfur and mist hung in the air. I had to see. I took a few steps across the threshold of the door, looked to my left and saw. Big Jim was snoring away, still in a coma as the smoky remnants of the blast continued to rise from beneath his bed.

He was a sleeper. But the snapshots of my dear friend, Mike, whom I have known for over forty years, and whose propensity it is to engage in Rumplestilskin-like siestas, are some of my favorites.

I had just purchased my first car, a souped-up 1968 Camaro with a worn, pale-blue paint job and four hundred fifty hungry horses pounding beneath its hood. It didn't look like much, but it was essentially built to be more rocket ship than automobile. My garage was the streets of the Bronx, and while I didn't live in the rough and tumble *barrios* of the South Bronx, it still was what it was. In other words, one leaving a hot rod on the street overnight without an armed guard attending to it, or at least an angry poodle sleeping within it, was likely to be *hot-rod-less* in due time.

Which is what I was just three weeks after I bought the thing.

I was horrified, of course, to return one early, beautiful Sunday morning to where I had parked my vehicle just the night before and find nothing more than an empty spot and the shattered remains of a driver's side window.

The remedy, I can assure you, was not to call the police, who would dutifully take a report and accomplish little else. I was still streetwise, then. I knew that local car thieves would often remove the vehicles they stole to certain sections of the neighborhood, strip them, and leave the remains as buzzards might leave the bones of carrion. I had one of these locations in mind and if I could get there quickly enough, well, there might be a chance I could retrieve my car. Or a significant portion of it.

Mike knew this as well, and he was the only one of the two of us still with vehicular transportation. I ran back to my house – a block away – and made a desperate call to him at about 9.00 that morning.

Mike was dead asleep when he picked up the phone. Meaning not that he *had been* asleep, but that he *was* asleep when he answered.

There are some of us, you see, for whom the demarcation between sleeping and wakefulness is clear and distinct. For others, however, the line is blurred and somewhat ambiguous. For such people, talking and walking and doing all manner of things while sleeping is neither impractical nor uncommon.

It was sometimes difficult to talk to Mike when he was in such a stupor. We conversed nevertheless; I informed him of recent events and he agreed to pick me up in fifteen minutes so we could search for the remains of my car.

I went downstairs and waited on the steps leading to my twenty-story apartment building. And I waited. Mike lived only about six blocks away, so it couldn't take him long to arrive. Could it?

I was pacing by 9:30 and talking to myself by 9:45. I returned to my apartment and called Mike once more.

He was still asleep. He didn't remember speaking to me. He was horrified that my car had been stolen. He agreed to come over in fifteen minutes, pick me up, and help me search for my car.

I went downstairs and waited on the steps again. And I waited.

At 10:15, I let my head slump into my hands, which seemed at the time a reasonable substitute for my mother holding me and rocking me.

At 10:30, those hands were smacking that head over and over, as if to wake *me* up – or *him* up *through* me, if that were possible – or to somehow purge from my brain the unnerving sense of unreality that began to overwhelm me. At 10:45, I returned to my apartment to call Mike. The conversation went something like this:

"Mike! Where are you?"

"Who is this?"

"Who is this? Is that what you said?"

"Dave?"

"Yes, it's friggin' Dave. Where are you?"

"What do you mean?"

"What do I mean? My car's been stolen!"

"You're kidding."

I'll spare you the rest. In sum, he had no memory of our two prior conversations. Indeed, why would he? He was asleep. Yet, he did promise to come over in fifteen minutes, pick me up, and help me search for my car.

Would you believe that I returned to the front of my building for a third time? I did.

I went downstairs and sat down and waited on the concrete steps leading to my apartment building, wondering all the while whether the stone and rock I was sitting upon might be more responsive than my dear friend.

I waited. Mike lived only about six blocks away, so it couldn't take him long to arrive.

Except, he never did. At 11:45, I returned to my apartment for good. I didn't call Mike; I called the police. They dutifully took a report. Predictably, my car was never seen nor heard of again.

That was the first time, but not the last time that Michael's exceptional *siestability* would be on full display.

We were in our early twenties, and we were going to a club called *Mother's*. Mother's was in the State of New Jersey, but Mike and I planned to be in a state no twenty-something should attempt to emulate.

We were small guys, you understand. It didn't take a lot to get us drunk, and we knew this. Thus, we could usually be relied upon to limit our drinking. We would typically have one or two, gawk at the women, talk to none, and leave empty-handed. These were objectives we were fully prepared to accomplish at Mother's.

We got to the club, had two drinks, gawked at the women, and talked to none. Having stared out the required period of gawk and having consumed our standard issue of alcohol, we turned to leave. But, someone caught Mike's eye on the way out.

I suppose a blonde, twenty-one-year-old girl with huge breasts and a red miniskirt, stumbling around a dark club at one in the morning on five-inch heels, and oblivious to the fact she was spilling her Bloody Mary all over her hand with every step she took, is someone any young American male would be instantly attracted to. Mike was no exception. He deserted me without hesitation and began to engage in a rambling conversation with her. Each time she was called upon to respond to one of his queries, she appeared to stagger, lurch forward, and catch his shoulder for support. Both charmed and encouraged, Mike ordered her a drink. He ordered one for himself. I ordered a shot of tequila and leaned against the wall drinking until he was finished failing with the chick.

It took twenty more minutes for him to do so which was, to his credit, much longer than usual. He returned to my side. I nodded to him in acknowledgment of his startling success, and we left. We were far from blind drunk, but we were both a bit buzzed. And it was late, and a long drive back home.

As we entered the car, I fulfilled my basic civic duty and checked on the condition of my friend who was the designated driver for the evening.

We were innovative even then. At that time, not enough people had been killed by drunk drivers for that phrase to exist.

I asked him if he was all right to drive. He said he was. I asked if he was sure. He said, "absolutely." I looked at him hesitantly. He appeared fine. I wasn't convinced. He reassured me. I told him I intended to take a little nap. He said that was *absolutely* fine, not to worry.

So, I proceeded to doze, and I didn't worry. I curled up into a ball in the passenger seat and closed my eyes, glad that I wasn't the one who had to drive. I began to drift quietly off to sleep, and I would have drifted quite a distance had it not been for the Gremlin.

The Gremlin is what I call that little voice that speaks to us all sometimes. It's that soft whisper that creeps into your ear every now and then. Call it a second thought, or second sight, or a nagging feeling, or something that otherwise lies buried in your subconscious, sitting patiently and biding its time, waiting for its moment, a moment when it will be heard.

Undoubtedly, there are many different kinds of Gremlins inhabiting us. Some are beneficial, and some are not. Some speak louder than others. Some are a lot smarter and seem to be correct more often.

That was the Gremlin that awoke and whispered three words to me just as I began to fall into a deep and soundless slumber. Here is what it said: *"Look at Mike."*

I swear. The Gremlin said that. Those were its words and they floated across my brain like some kind of newsflash on those electronic banners in Times Square.

So I did what the Gremlin suggested and opened my eyes.

I don't know what reached my sensory array first; whether it was the sight of Mike with his eyes closed, or his head slumped against his right shoulder, or the deep rumble of his fitful snore as he dreamed of Bloody Marys and half-naked women. I just don't know. I can say that the sight of these things frightened me very, very much, enough to jolt me to a state of instant wakefulness with a burst of adrenaline that could have launched the Apollo.

Without more than a moment's thought – and realizing that our combined life spans could easily be measured in that space of time – I clenched my left hand into a fist, arched it across my body, and pounded that fist as hard as I could into the center of his chest, as if I were attempting to restart the heart of a dead man. In many ways, this was exactly what I was trying to accomplish.

Needless to say, he did awake, shaking his head and blinking his eyes in bewilderment as if he had just been disassembled by one of Captain Kirk's transporters and beamed right into his car in the middle of the night. He looked to his left, then at me. I wasn't sure he recognized me. I wasn't sure he knew where he was. Or who he was.

As is my nature, my comments to him were brief and to the point. "Damn it, Mike, you fell asleep!"

"You're kidding?" was his only reply.

It's important to note that this story is amusing only because we survived. While we all know the stories of people who consume a gallon of vodka and proceed to drive the wrong way down the freeway, please remember that even casual or controlled drinking can produce fatal results. I've found it is best not to have to rely on your inner Gremlin to warn you in the nick of time.

Hey, you want to have a lot of snapshots, don't you?

No Knack For The Kayak

IT REALLY STARTED as I planned my family's summer vacation in Kitty Hawk, North Carolina, and when I called my old pal, Tom, who is a native of that state.

I'm always concerned about the weather when we take our annual vacations and I was particularly concerned about the possibility – however remote – of extreme weather. Specifically, I inquired about the likelihood of a hurricane in August.

"Early August, Dave?" my dear friend asked with his ever-present drawl. "Way too early for a hurricane," he said. "You should be fine."

Of course, we were fine, even after Hurricane Alex, which struck the North Carolina coastline on August 3, 2004, where we sat in our rented beach house as winds reached eighty miles per hour, and the structure swayed back and forth on stilts that provided significant protection against high tides, but none at all against hurricane-force winds.

Or perhaps it all *truly* began the day after the hurricane. After the winds had died down to a mere twenty-five miles an hour and after most of the clouds had cleared from the sky with the passing storm. It was breezy, but all in all, a beautiful day, and the sun shone brightly in the warm North Carolina air.

Let me explain something: We were on a vacation. My family *does* stuff when we're on vacation. This is so despite my wife's irrational and oft-communicated desire to just park her body upon the beaches our hotels are frequently located behind and slowly fry the day away under the sun.

So, despite my wife's proclivities, we go rock climbing so that we can say we risk our lives at least once each year. We go snorkeling, where I try my hand at drowning, and my daughters feign concern and commence half-hearted attempts at rescue. We go hiking, in an attempt to attract the attention of local newshounds looking for a small piece about naive tourists getting lost on a mountaintop.

This time we went kayaking. We had planned for it, we'd paid for it in advance, it was a nice day and we were going. It was a guided little jaunt on the bayside of that strip of barrier islands called the Outer Banks which forms the North Carolina coastline, with an experienced kayaker taking lead of a small group of intrepid boaters.

What I call the "bayside" was Kitty Hawk Bay. Kitty Hawk Bay is a picturesque little body of water that empties into the Albemarle Sound. Albemarle Sound doesn't carry with it the potential thrills of the wide-open Atlantic, but there are twelve miles between its northern and southern shores and it extends about fifty miles inland from the ocean.

Have you ever seen anything fifty miles away? Unless you were in an aircraft or a skyscraper or on a mountaintop, probably not. Of course, at the time, the precise dimensions of the sound were of little concern to me.

My daughter, Ariana – ten years old at the time – would be with me in one kayak. My eldest, Stephanie, along for the ride with her somewhat less-than-athletically-inclined mother would be in another.

"How hard can it be?" queried my lovely bride.

Indeed. Well, we would all have life jackets. The primary function of these devices, I have always thought, is to facilitate the job of rescuers, by ensuring that dead bodies remain floating on the surface of the water for timely retrieval and expedient disposal.

But, as I've stated, we were on vacation, and it was no place for bleak fantasies or runaway imaginings. "How hard can it be?" I asked myself in my mind.

I was in pretty good shape, after all, well-rested after a night of storm watching and so what if my left arm was practically useless because of a rotator cuff injury?

We'd be fine. Piece of cake. Guided. Bayside. Life jackets. No problem.

A kayak, as you may know, is not exactly a rowboat, although that's probably its closest nautical relation. It's a thin slice of a boat, equipped with paddles, not oars. It's designed for two to scull along in a coordinated fashion. This coordination can be fairly critical to the smooth and efficient operation of the craft and the possible difficulties inherent in coordinating such a function with two pubescent daughters did not occur to me.

A kayak is also more maneuverable and lighter than a rowboat. Also, easier to tip over and fall from. Thus, the life jackets.

Hey… Bayside. Guided. Piece of cake.

We suited up and began – a small group of us – led by a handsome, muscular, overly pleasant, tanned, bearded twenty-something who looked like a participant in *The Survivor* TV series.

Ariana and I took the first boat. It took only a few seconds to realize that we were being pulled from the dock and into the bay by incredibly strong currents left over from the prior night's storm. My fellow kayakers, led by our intrepid guide, seemed oblivious to our difficulties as they headed north – towards protected shallows and marshes – with little trouble.

I struggled just to shout strangled orders to my brave and self-reliant offspring. She was doing her level best to be a good sailor and dutifully obey her captain. She undoubtedly hoped that if I decided to go down with my ship, I wouldn't insist she accompany me.

As the pain in my injured shoulder steadily mounted, I realized not only that we had traveled just a few feet from the dock, but that our combined efforts were barely enough to maintain that distance for much longer. I summoned a last burst of adrenaline and managed to close the distance between our boat and the wooden pier, desperately grabbed on to it, and pulled the kayak alongside.

I looked up and saw the guide about fifty feet away, staring at us with some bemusement. I made a slash across my throat with my left hand. We were done. "We're done," I shouted.

I climbed weakly onto the dock and helped my daughter do the same. The guide slowly paddled towards us with a look on his face that suggested this had never happened before.

However, so concerned was I with our immediate survival, that the thought of my wife and eldest daughter had not entered my mind for several minutes. I looked around. They were nowhere to be seen. They certainly couldn't have disappeared into thin air and we hadn't been in the water that long, so they must be close by, right?

Right.

I looked around, with greater urgency now, as the guide approached.

Nothing.

I scanned the surrounding marshes, picked out each kayak one by one and subjected each to a closer examination. My remaining family members were not among them.

With my heart pounding rapidly in my chest, I looked to the west, beyond the bay and into the sound, which, to me, looked no different than the open sea. And I saw.

Of course, exactly what I saw didn't register at first, mainly because a small dot in the distance is not immediately recognizable as any familiar form. I squinted and shaded my eyes for a better view. Small dots of perspiration appeared instantly on my brow and my breath quickened.

It couldn't be. No way!

But, it was. Somehow, in some way, Stephanie and Andrea, along with their stalwart vessel, had been pulled by the currents deep into the Albemarle Sound, possibly to a distance of a half-mile away. I had no reason to believe that they wouldn't continue to be pulled deeper and deeper into the sound and farther and farther from the shore.

I knew – I mean, I absolutely *knew* – that there was no possible way I could rescue them. This was so despite the fact that my inner nature carries with it the potential for great heroics, as I hope this journal faithfully attests.

Put another way, they were dead.

I turned to Ariana and put a comforting hand on her shoulders.

"Your mother and sister are lost to the sea, sweetheart," I quipped, not thinking I had quipped at all.

It was then that the pleasant, soft-spoken and mild-mannered Neanderthal who functioned as our guide arrived at the dock in his kayak. He carried a look of wonder upon his countenance. It pushed through the bushy confines of his beard, the hairs of which started from the dizzying heights of his cheekbones and continued without break or pause down his face, neck, and shirtless chest and abdomen until, having nowhere else to go, meandered – with somewhat less luxuriousness – all over his back.

I got down to business with him immediately. I pointed sharply with my left hand to the western horizon.

"Retrieve my wife, please," I commanded politely. I really didn't want to see whether he would accept the challenge or whether he would be successful if he did.

In any case, I was thinking far past those possible events, wondering whether there was a nearby Coast Guard station, equipped with a helicopter. I turned to Ariana once more and placed another comforting hand on her shoulder.

"They're gone, darling. We must find a way to go on," I said. She smiled weakly. I looked to the sky and held my breath.

This story, like most of those that you'll read here, has a happy ending. About twenty minutes later, the guide cheerfully paddled into the area around the dock with my wife's kayak in tow, attached by a rope to his. He paddled rhythmically, calmly, and with little discernible effort, making him appear quite super-human, and making me appear grossly inadequate as a husband, as a father, and as a man.

My wife reclined in rather elegant fashion on the rear seat of the boat as if she didn't have a care in the world. There was a broad smile upon her face. She wore a large straw hat to shield her delicate features from the southern sun and was missing only the obligatory blade of tufted grass between her lips, painting a rather idyllic picture of the whole affair.

Stephanie was jumping up and down in the front of the boat, screaming and gesticulating wildly, obviously overjoyed to be reunited with her father and grateful for his role, however small, in her timely rescue.

As the convoy passed before me, I heard my beloved daughter's words. Every other had four letters.

She was twelve at the time. But she was almost thirteen.

"This isn't so bad," my wife remarked pleasantly, as Stephanie continued her venom-spewed rant and the pair continued their chauffeured ride past the point where I was standing on the dock. It became clear to me that the guide was fully prepared to continue the tour in just this fashion.

Needless to say, I was embarrassed by my daughter's choice of verbiage, and mortified by my wife's stark and easy acquiescence – in the context of this wholly disastrous outing – to transport by human caveman through the watery wilderness of the marshland, as if she were some kind of amphibious pampered poodle. Furthermore, I was humiliated by my lack of physical strength and my wholly deficient leadership skills. I declined to take the guide's implied offer of *caravan-ness* and put an end to the entire charade. I collected my family and humbly returned to my car with my tail beneath my legs; physically exhausted, emotionally drained, my injured shoulder on fire and $200 poorer.

It occurs to me as I write, that each of my family members has told this story somewhat differently.

In short, Stephanie has always insisted that her mother refused to paddle, compelling her to bear the entire burden of transport by herself. She states that her mother's sole contribution, as the currents pulled them deeper and deeper into the oblivion of the sound, was to command her repeatedly to *"Head to terra firma!"*

My wife denies these allegations in the entirety. She is adamant that it was her loving daughter's manic refusal to accept the wise advice of her dear mother that was responsible for their plight.

My youngest is always the intellectual. She is perfectly willing to accept that her mother's and sister's rank incompetence, lack of coordination and scarcity of discipline were the direct causes of their predicament. However, she's incapable of explaining her father's astounding physical failings and pitiful lack of command, which she can't excuse merely because of his deteriorating physical condition and failing mental state, both of which naturally accompany his advanced age.

The Autograph

MY FATHER, rest his soul, was the treasurer of a large construction company located on Long Island. He was a respected, influential voice in the company, and quietly, but forcefully, directed its financial affairs for decades before his death. He was a consummate conservative in this regard, extremely disciplined in all ways, and his mind was largely uncluttered by minutia and triviality.

But, Dad had another side to him, and the contents of his impressive office – complete with a bathroom; a big deal in those days – belied his otherwise conservative nature. Because it was packed with toys of one kind or another.

What I mean by "toys" are *things* – doodads, souvenirs, mementos and talismans – that were present for the amusement and comfort of the occupant alone. These included a rather ugly fig tree Dad had grown from a seed; a model of an apartment house that his company had built; and a human skull.

Also, an autographed baseball located on the shelf behind his desk, unceremoniously displayed without plaque, casing or description of any kind. It was a pitted, yellowed and clearly ancient piece of memorabilia. It contained a number of signatures in ink faded by the years. The names there ranged from the famous to the unknown, including Babe Ruth, Joe DiMaggio, "Crazy Legs" Dimeo and others.

As the story goes, my father was hosting a meeting in his office with a number of suits, undoubtedly discussing the intricate detail of a multi-million dollar project, when one of the participants noticed the ball. He asked to inspect it close-up, a request my father obliged. The man studied it carefully, visibly impressed.

"This is amazing," he said.

"Yes, it is," my father replied.

"Where did you get this?"

"I've had it for a long, long time."

"You have Babe Ruth's signature, here."

"I do."

"And Mickey Mantle's."

"Yes."

"You also have Lou Gehrig's autograph."

"Yes, I do."

"There's just one thing."

"What's that?"

"Isn't "Gehrig" spelled G-E-H-R-I-G?"

"Is it?"

"Yes."

"OK."

"But, the signature on this ball spells it G-E-R-I-G."

"Does it?"

"Yeah."

"Let me see."

With that, my father examined the ball and wisely nodded his head, agreeing with his colleague. He then picked up a pen, added an "H" to the signature in the appropriate place, and returned it to the businessman.

Stunned, it didn't take much longer for the man to realize that the ball was a forgery and that my father had signed each and every name on the ball himself.

Revelation

IT WAS JULY, 2011, and my family was on vacation on the island of St. Maarten. My children and my wife were sleeping their holiday away, as is sometimes their preference, and I was walking alone on a deserted beach early in the morning, as is sometimes my preference on such island excursions.

I was also despondent. The reasons why aren't important. Let's say that my head was filled with questions that had no answers. Or that I was concerned for my future, or troubled about my past, or worried about the health of my children, or distracted by any one of the struggles that plague so many of us.

Thunderheads threatened the morning sky and matched my dark state of mind. As I strolled, the beach became more isolated; the homes fewer and farther apart. The shells on the beach became more exotic and plentiful, as there were fewer people to scoop them up. I became more downhearted as I walked.

My gloomy mood warped into a weird kind of resignation; a surrender of sorts. This was ridiculous because I was on vacation, hell, I was in the *Caribbean* – and at no small expense, either – but I just couldn't help it. I began to talk to myself, determined to reason a way out of my mental morass. I said to myself – quite irrationally or desperately perhaps – that my problems would resolve themselves in a few steps. I steadfastly determined that in just a few more steps, the answers I sought would present themselves to me right there on that beach. I walked on, talking to myself out loud, repeating this phrase: "…any step now…I'll have my answer in just a few steps…"

At that moment, my eyes fixed on a small shell lying on the beach. I bent down, picked it up and examined it. It was just a scrap of shell, only a small piece of the home some sea animal had created for itself, yet it had an unusual color and an intricate shape. Without thinking at all, I exclaimed, "How beautiful."

I realized, almost at once that I had the answer I sought. That answer had been contained in a tiny piece of irregularly shaped calcium shaped by a long dead creature, one of the thousands and thousands whose former residences littered the beach.

Santayana said that the earth has music for those who will listen. But, at various moments in our lives, we're incapable of hearing the melody. We become overwhelmed by our problems. They force our eyes closed and make us blind to the small wonders of this world. They seal our ears and make us deaf to songs that are always there, but that at times may be little more than soft whispers floating on ocean breezes.

We can easily forget that we are all embraced by the harmonies of this earth. We can forget that we're are blessed with good things in our lives and that we are surrounded, everywhere, by the divine music of this world.

It is there for those of us who choose to hear.

Free Bird

THERE AREN'T TOO MANY MOMENTS in a man's life when he finds himself face to face with a revelation.

If you're paying attention, you will recognize such a moment. It will be rare, and fleeting. It will contain something pure, something ethereal; a message from somewhere else, from somewhere outside, delivered without effort or pretense; not shouted from a mountaintop, or propelled across a lectern, or whispered into your ear by a spirit. It will be an inspiration that travels along a moonbeam, like a sigh murmured softly upon the trail of a whisper.

There will be no witnesses to attest to its happening other than you. There may be no hard evidence or objective fact that will explain its significance. What you experience at this moment will defy anyone's lofty opinions or scrupulous analysis. You won't be able to convert it to a formula, or make a religion out of it, or name it, or cure depression with it, or use it to pick a winner in the stock market.

But you will understand its message. If you allow it, it will change you.

In the early 1990s, I rented a house with my young family in Yorktown Heights, New York. It was a small, but neat ranch house, situated on a steep hill that sloped downward to a one-quarter acre backyard. In the yard was a thicket of wild blueberry bushes. The bushes grew so dense that it took me days to mow a meandering path through the four-foot high plants. The lower level of the home contained one large room that I used as a study. It had a door that led to a stone patio overlooking the backyard.

It was a brutally hot summer day, during a brutally hot summer. Temperatures had exceeded 100 degrees for almost a week. As I was reading in the relative coolness of the room, I took a momentary break and rose to gaze at the relaxing greenery of the yard. Instead, on the slate of the patio, I saw a blackbird lying on its side in the stultifying heat. It had no visible injuries, but it was easy to see that the recent weather had been the bird's downfall. It didn't look as if it would survive.

Wishing to mitigate the animal's suffering if I could, I found a small cardboard box and lined it with a cloth. I donned a pair of work gloves, gently removed the bird from the sizzling stone floor of the patio, and placed it in the box in the coolness of my study.

I watched it, whispering to it gently. The bird was breathing – barely – but other than that seemed incapable of moving. It was just an ordinary blackbird, but there wasn't a mark on it that dulled or marred its feathers. Its simple beauty touched me and I was terribly distressed that I had been chosen to witness its final moments.

I stepped away for a few seconds to return my gloves to their proper place and returned grimly to watch the poor thing die. When I did, I realized that the bird had stopped breathing and that in the brief moment of my absence, it had quietly passed away.

But it had stirred before it died. What it had done, this small and insignificant creature, in some inexplicable way – while just a moment before, incapable of making the slightest movement or resisting the efforts of another small and insignificant creature who, in an act of kindness and pity, had removed it to a more comfortable place in which to spend its last moments on earth – what it had done was to spread its wings wide-open, as if it were about to fly away to some other place.

Perhaps it did.

How an animal thinks, I suppose none of us can truly know. That it perceives the world and its place in this vale differently and through a more narrow and clouded lens than do you and I seems clear.

They say that animals don't think of the future or the past but that they live in the moment. They don't complicate their brief lives contemplating the meaning of their existence or fearing their eventual demise, or wondering whether there is a world beyond this one, or of any other of the *what-ifs* of their lives. Yet, for all of this, they seem to perceive things that you and I cannot or will not; things that our oversized brains somehow seem incapable of grasping.

Many of us carry our faith close to our hearts. Many of us believe that there is a life after this one and that we do go someplace when we pass. We *believe* this without being able to truly *know*. After all, we always seem to be lacking some objective *proof* of a hereafter. Perhaps it is that the true meaning of the word "faith" is that we shouldn't require any.

But every rare once in a while, we are given exactly that. Now and then there *is* proof right before our eyes, corroboration that our intellect or our reasoning often doesn't allow us to accept.

Maybe this evidence will come to us in the wondrous guise of a small sea creature's home on a beach. Maybe it will come in the form of a blackbird spreading its wings as it dies.

I do not know. But I don't think I have to *know*. All I have to do is imagine what that blackbird might have seen just as it passed away.

The Lie-mo-zeene

AROUND 1980 and one year out of Boston University, I applied for a job as a writer for a small magazine in Monterey, California. They responded, and proposed a trial run of sorts, offering to fly me out there and hire me for a week. My trip would be fully paid for; airline tickets would be sent to me, and a limousine would pick me up at the airport.

This was a particularly impressive thing to say to a 24-year-old. A limousine would pick me up at the airport! Was I friggin' *important* or what?

I hoped my father would be impressed by this. I had a rocky relationship with him sometimes, but we were a small and close-knit family. Gaining his approval was important to me.

Excited, I rushed to tell him the news.

I did, and he laughed at me.

Well, that's not quite true. He laughed *hysterically* at me. Like some omnipresent comedian, he predicted through chokes of laughter that a limousine would certainly *not* be picking me up at the airport.

This statement, as you can imagine, confounded me. I was told that a limousine would pick me up at the airport. My father disagreed. And, he was laughing at me. I requested that he enlighten me, and in response he explained: it was a *"lie-mo-zeene"* that would be retrieving me. This did not clarify his previous statement nor explain his mirth. I asked for further clarification, which my father happily provided.

A "limousine," he explained, was a long, stretchy-type vehicle; luxurious, beautiful, often black or white, and the kind of conveyance taken only to funerals, weddings and the like. A limousine would not be greeting me. What *would* be there waiting for me at the Monterey airport was a "lie-mo-zeene." In other words, a taxicab.

I thought it strange that my father would make such a prediction and that he had crafted such an odd, prophetic distinction between the vehicle I expected and the vehicle that might be waiting for me. I thought I had conveyed some rather extraordinary news: information that just *had* to impress a parent who was typically hard to impress.

In any event, sometime later, I found myself in an airport in California, waiting for my prearranged ride to take me to my prearranged hotel. I wish I could say that I was completely surprised when the "lie-mo-zeene" came to get me.

It was a caricature of itself, an ancient, battered relic of a vehicle, so old that it was impossible to identify its make or model or even its country of origin. Or planet of origin.

As it approached, the first thing I saw were the white felt *dingo balls* dangling in the car's interior, running along the perimeter of the front windshield. The second thing I saw was a bright-blue figurine, ten inches tall with flowing black hair, affixed to the center of the dashboard. I couldn't identify it precisely because its back was turned to me. As the figure's two broad arms were outstretched, I thought for sure it must be a model of Jesus Christ. Until I noticed that its hands were balled into fists and that one fist was grasping a microphone, which I thought was strange. I mean, it *could* have been a statuette of Jesus Christ. But, more than likely, it was one of Ozzie Osbourne. I took a deep breath.

The car shuddered to a stop in a cloud of blue smoke, accompanied by the pungent aroma of burning oil. I wished I hadn't taken a deep breath. I saw that the car's tires were stripped bare, as if treads were superfluous luxuries here. The front bumper – containing more rust than chrome – appeared to be hanging from the buggy by a magical and invisible thread. Its body was painted an orange-red and pitted everywhere with irregular patches of rust-brown. In a strange way, it reminded me of a giraffe on wheels.

I chuckled involuntarily. Then the chuckle froze on my lips. I became transfixed and stood and gaped at the car. The driver opened his window and smiled broadly, proudly displaying what could only be described as unfortunate bridgework, installed with a reckless abandon. He held up a small placard with my name printed on it. He didn't ask whether the name on the card belonged to me; he seemed to know already. Which made him pretty amazing. Also, patient. He waited for me to close my mouth.

As I opened the rear passenger door, I was greeted by an interior colored a bright red worthy of Superman's cape. The plastic of the rear seat was complete with a huge slash across its center that exposed the yellow foam rubber within, and that bulged from it like some kind of man-made hernia.

Some time passed.

Eventually, the short, middle-aged driver with the charming bridgework gently removed the suitcase from my left hand. I was still standing with the rear door wide-open, staring, and didn't have the strength to resist. He seemed to understand completely and removed himself to the trunk, where he released the lid with a terrifying shriek of metal rubbing on metal. I was momentarily overwhelmed by the smell of gasoline. Ultimately, I sat down in the rear seat gingerly, composed myself, and smiled.

Sometimes I was amazed at how *right* my father could be. That this event caused so distinct a memory for both father and son was never really understood; except, perhaps, to prove Dad's point that he was some kind of prophet, possessed of certain senses so keen, and instincts so acute, as to practically convert him to the status of soothsayer.

Sewer Covers Hover

I WAS DRIVING ONE SUMMER on the Long Island Expressway, that notorious byway familiar to all New Yorkers and known simply by the acronym "LIE." It flows through most of the 150 mile length of Long Island, the peninsular suburbia extending eastward from New York City.

There is a mile-long section of that roadway in the Borough of Queens that crosses what was at one time swampland. It's adjacent to Flushing Meadows Park, the site of the 1964 World's Fair. Here, the road's elevation decreases dramatically.

Several curious appurtenances can be found embedded in the asphalt along this short stretch of road, objects so commonplace to city-folk that few would notice they were there at all. They are noteworthy not for *what* they are, but for *where* they are.

New York City sewer covers (also known as "manhole covers") are circular iron discs measuring about 25 inches across and weighing upwards of one hundred pounds. They allow entry from the surface to the interior of what are really storm drains, but that everyone called, and for all I know still call "sewers." At the same time, they effectively prevent access to all but those individuals possessing a sturdy iron bar, terrific strength, and the courage to encounter *God knows what the hell might be down there.*

When we were kids, we'd play stickball on the crowded streets. Stickball – just one derivation of the game of baseball – is played, well, with a stick and a ball. The "stick" is typically your common broomstick without the broom: the ball is a sphere of pink rubber commonly referred to as a Spaldeen.

Cars, always parked on either side of the street, substituted as bases. As you may imagine, a typical city street is much narrower than any Little League baseball field and the outfield goes on forever because no New York City street ever ends. That said, balls would invariably pass by one of us. Following gravity, they would find their way into those iron-rimmed rectangular jaws found on every street corner. Which were the sewers.

No one wanted to lose the ball down the sewers because that could end the game. Fortunately, the balls never really *went* anywhere; at least not right away. They would land about five feet down those dark, black holes and float in the center of an indescribable muck, often next to the remains of some dead rodent.

You aren't eating as you read this, I hope?

If the water level was high enough, someone slight of frame – like me – could slide through the sewer, head first, and grab the ball. In this event, my sole safety net was the most reliable lad among us. He would hold my legs as I stretched my arm, held my breath, and tried to ignore the *Daliesque unreality* of placing my head in a sewer. Difficult to ignore was the alien-like slime coating the ball when I retrieved it.

If the water level was low, a different problem presented. There were ladders in there, you know, leading to the iron covers at street level. The trick was to enter the sewer completely, without any safety net, grab the ladder, climb down deeper into the hole, retrieve the ball and get yourself out of there as quickly as possible. That was a surreal experience, too, and we had all heard about the alligators living down there. But, being kids – and being kids from the Bronx – we would push that out of our minds and forge ahead.

Hey, we had to get the ball.

Back to the story: There are sewer covers on every New York City street, but they simply do not exist in the center lanes of any major highway. Except, on one short stretch of road on the Long Island Expressway.

I was driving down this highway, on this certain stretch of road and, though I am somewhat reluctant to admit it, I was rolling a joint as I drove.

I wasn't *inhaling*, of course, you sillies. That would be both illegal and potentially perilous.

But you may be curious as to how I could operate my vehicle when both of my hands were rolling a joint and I will be happy to explain. I was *doing the knee*, a phrase coined by one of my dearest friends, Stacey. This practice permits your knee to control the steering wheel, freeing the two fine hands God gave you, and allowing them to accomplish more pressing tasks.

Over the years, I've had the opportunity to reflect upon some of the things I did when I was a bit younger. I truly have no excuse for some of them, except to concede that somewhere within me there lies a bottomless well of stupidity and that I drink from it from time to time, depending upon how thirsty I am. The truth hurts, as they say, but I do wish to be honest with you all if, for no other reason than responsible parents may use this book as a primer to teach children what they should never do at any time.

I was getting off the highway the very next exit, anyway. And, none of this had anything to do with what happened next.

I should mention that it's easy to drive a car when you're rolling a joint, but it's rather difficult to roll a joint while you're driving a car. It really does take a bit of concentration, as well as an innate facility to multi-task.

Be that as it may, and as challenging as the undertaking may be, you do have to look up sometime, just to see how the road has been doing while you were away.

That time came, and when it did, I looked up. What I saw was a sewer cover floating in the air about thirty feet above me.

Yes, you heard right. It was floating in the air.

I am not describing an act of magic or sorcery, of course, and you may have seen this demonstrated before in one major motion picture starring Bruce Willis. The iron disc was being held aloft by a remarkably powerful jet stream of water blasting from the sewer itself. Municipal employees unintentionally provided the explanation for this rare occurrence when they arrived at the scene after the event had concluded of its own accord.

As I've stated, the area was low lying, and there had been an unusually heavy rain just hours before. When these circumstances combine, the storm drain system becomes overloaded – more water passes through the system than it's designed to handle – and all that water eventually has to go somewhere. It seeks the weakest point of egress, as water tends to do, and then travels where it wishes; in this case, straight up.

So, there the sewer cover remained, suspended in the air, and by the time I noticed it, I was only a few yards away. Let me tell you, at 60 miles an hour, a few yards come and go quite rapidly.

The sewer cover didn't hover very long, either. As Newton taught us so well, what goes up must come down. In the space of a heartbeat, this impressive flying disc – known to me intimately from those parts of my childhood previously related – began its downward trajectory. I was on an intercept course. In other words, I was traveling directly into its path and could well imagine what might occur if I crossed it.

I grabbed the steering wheel instantly and veered to my left, the half-rolled joint still in my left hand. In the space of another heartbeat, I heard a somewhat horrifying crash above my head. I could easily deduce what had caused it.

The Gods of the Highway were not through with me yet, at least not without a bit more sport. One heartbeat later, a second sewer cover exploded from the road in front of me: this one propelled by a similar jet spray but floating at a much more reasonable height of about twelve feet. Not wishing to dally, it commenced its descent almost as quickly as it had ascended.

This second disc – now a deadly, life-threatening projectile – crashed through my windshield like a Frisbee, inexplicably stretching the glass before breaking it, and it came to a halt as it met the headrest of the passenger side seat.

Had someone been sitting in that seat, that poor soul would have been neatly decapitated before my eyes, and this tale would be neither amusing nor, in all likelihood, told to you at all. Somebody would have sued someone for millions and collected, I am sure. I would have been traumatized for life, and that life, I'm also sure, would have been dramatically different from the one I ultimately had.

I managed to drive off my intended exit just yards ahead – shaking like the proverbial leaf – and pulled my car to the side of the service road. I exited with shaky knees, looking at the condition of my vehicle with some amazement. One sewer cover was inside the car: the other had landed upon its now obliterated rooftop.

At that moment, I noticed a man crossing the street and coming towards me. He was stumbling more than walking and looked as if he had smoked *dozens* of joints just moment before. He stopped and gaped.

"What happened?" he asked in fair amazement. On the one hand, I felt the answer to his question was stupidly obvious. On the other hand, I found his query sufficiently complex enough to stump Solomon himself. Somewhat exasperated, I simply stated the obvious: "Sewer covers," I said.

"*New York City* sewer covers?" he asked.

"Apparently," I replied.

He approached my car in disbelief and then extended his right hand. I looked down at his hand with some disbelief of my own. Then, reflexively, I shook it.

"Congratulations, my brother!" he said with authentic delight. "You're a millionaire!"

He proceeded to leave the scene – a decent soul, apparently – genuinely pleased by my good fortune, and no doubt wishing he had been as lucky as me. I returned to my car, leaned against the driver's side door, folded my arms, and waited to see what would happen next. After all, it was perfectly clear to me by that time, that all of this had been planned by a higher power and that this play was being scripted in the entirety for some cosmic purpose

I had yet to divine. I didn't have to wait long.

Moments later, a huge hook and ladder fire truck, with a dozen firemen clinging to its frame, pulled alongside my vehicle and stopped. We sat there for a few moments, just staring at each other, which was understandable, I suppose, under the circumstances. Every mouth on that truck was wide-open. Every set of eyes was in a similar state. No one said a word for a few minutes. Finally, one of the firemen spoke up.

"We need the lids," were all the words he could manage.

Now, no one had a cell phone in those days, you understand. There was no way of recording this event and it occurred to me immediately that if anyone removed the iron covers from where they resided, no one on God's earth would believe what had just happened. If I attempted to relate this tale to anyone, I would either be committed to an institution or convicted of insurance fraud. I conveyed my reluctance to part with either of my two souvenirs just yet.

His only response was to turn and point to the thoroughfare from which I had just exited. The highway had become a parking lot; the cars were backed up for what seemed like miles. It dawned on me that the reasons for this were obvious: there were two huge, perfectly round holes somewhere on that road that drivers would be reluctant to negotiate around. Further, it occurred to me that *my* two sewer covers were not the only ones in this space of roadway. Undoubtedly, those operators directly behind me, who had witnessed the event, were a bit reluctant to pass. At least, until they could be assured that the divine being that had caused all this had settled down a bit and was no longer so annoyed.

I allowed the firemen to retrieve their prizes, which they did with ginger trepidation and no small bit of reverence. After all, these things had been *alive* just a few moments ago, and I guess there was no telling what they might do next. When they left, I opened the driver's side door, sat down, and looked around.

My entire car was destroyed, except for a small area no larger than the width of my driver's side seat. This space had been somehow insulated from the cataclysm, as had the driver who had occupied it. My only injury was a small cut to the pinky of my left hand.

I must tell you that during all of this, the half-rolled joint fared rather well. I obviously survived not only to tell this tale, but to smoke the joint, which soon became a medicinal necessity, not a recreational distraction.

I don't know how all this could possibly have occurred the way that it did, but it did, and I imagine that stranger things have happened in a universe composed of a billion galaxies filled with procreating dinosaurs, black holes, and alien races.

It was also clear to me that Providence had been at work, and further, that it had taken on multiple tasks. I mean, it was difficult to figure out whether I had been lucky or unlucky. What were the odds of something like this happening? Of the tens of thousands of cars that traveled this road each day, what were the odds that it would happen to *me*? Furthermore, considering that it *had* happened, and happened to *me*, what were the odds I would *survive*?

A million to one, I guess. But I'm reminded of the saying that "a million to one" can sometimes be considered good odds.

If you're the *one*.

A Shot In The Dark

THE CAMPBELL APARTMENT is a highly ornate and remarkably beautiful cocktail lounge tucked into a discrete corner of the world-famous Grand Central Terminal in the heart of New York City. Legend has it that it was originally leased by an early twentieth-century tycoon, John Campbell, who used it as his private office simply to be physically closer to his investments. He ultimately abandoned it, and his office was sealed and forgotten until the terminal's massive renovation in the 1970s. Then, the room was unsealed, a New York architectural treasure was re-discovered, and an unfortunate homeless man who had been occupying the lavish space for years cruelly evicted.

It's also an expensive place to drink, as I discovered, particularly when one enjoys a good, single malt scotch now and then.

Always a rum or vodka drinker, I discovered single malts around 2012, and began my experimentation properly with a foray into the many offerings of The Macallan distillery, which will part with any of its bottles if you're willing to part with at least a fifty dollar bill. I would pop into Campbell's every once in a while and have a scotch or two before boarding the commuter train home. On one particular afternoon, I enjoyed a 12-year-old Macallan, and then enjoyed another, and then as was typical, turned to go. As I did, I noticed that the bar stocked numerous varieties of the brand and, in particular, a 25-year-old selection.

"Is that a 25-year-old Macallan I see?" I innocently inquired of the handsome bartender sporting a white formal shirt, a black vest, black bow tie and neatly slicked back hair.

"Yes, it is, sir," he replied.

Curious, and still a scotch neophyte, I eagerly replied, "Let's try the Macallan 25, then!" I was pleased with my obvious sophistication and taste, and clearly all those who overheard my selection were impressed, as well.

I should have sensed something as I watched the bartender pour from the sacred flagon. He steadied the bottle with his right hand, never removing it lest the flask somehow leap from his grip and shatter into a million pieces. His left hand sought out a silver-plated shot glass, apparently used to measure this stuff. Five minutes seemed to pass as he carefully poured the liquor into a crystal glass, refusing to allow a single drop of it to fall to the bar, or worse, linger somehow on the rim of the glass and evaporate into an unforgiving atmosphere.

When he was through, he cautiously placed the glass before me, rapidly glancing at me with a surreptitious narrowing of his eyes as if to ask whether he could trust me with such a spirit. Somehow convinced, he returned his gaze to the glass and slowly withdrew his hand. Apparently, this shot was to be vigilantly guarded until I took full possession of it.

I was terribly pleased by the entire display and quite awed with myself for bringing it about. I secured my drink; the bartender leaned back with a sigh of relief, and then spoke.

"That will be $82.36, sir," he said. He smiled.

I smiled back. I also took an involuntary step backward. I chuckled to myself, then stepped forward and coyly wiggled my index finger at the bartender, beckoning him to come a bit closer and indulge me with a brief conference.

"Did you say $82.36?" I asked into his ear.

"Yes, sir, I did," he replied into mine.

Now, mind you, I don't consider myself a cheap person and I've often been accused of throwing money around just for effect (or as I like to say, for the pure pleasure of it). I never minded paying twenty dollars a shot for a 12 year at the Campbell, even though I could have gone home and enjoyed my own shot for about three dollars.

Notwithstanding, I said the first thing that came to my mind, and the only thing possible to say under the circumstances: "You're friggin' kidding me, right?"

The bartender was impassive. "No, sir," he replied.

I took a *voluntary* step backward this time, knowing that this experience would somehow make itself into a small chapter in a book one day. It was also instantly eligible for my "stupidest things I have ever done" list.

I reached for my wallet and realized I had only a twenty-dollar bill remaining there. I removed the twenty and placed a credit card before the barkeep, as if it were an offering to the gods. I laughed quietly to myself. Humor and class are two qualities one should never leave home without, and I was fortunate to have both that day. I think. "Well, I ordered it, didn't I?" I asked.

"Yes, sir, you did," the bartender replied gamely, not quite sure where I was going with all this.

"And, you poured it, didn't you?"

"Yes, sir, I did."

"Well, if I can order an $82 shot of scotch," I replied, "I sure as hell can tip the bartender who brought it to me twenty dollars."

With that, I handed the bartender the twenty. He cracked up, as did his two associates behind the bar. I proceeded to enjoy my $102 shot of scotch, which I can assure you took less time to drink than to pour.

I never ordered the 25 year at Campbell's again, just like I can never order whiskey sours because I had four of them at a party once and threw up for three hours. Nevertheless, I had discovered something: Not only the far-reaching limits of my naiveté, but also that I had made three friends of three bartenders, who never again forgot that I drank Macallan..

But the 12 year variety, as I sometimes need to remind them to this day.

The Funniest Man On Earth

AS THE TITLE SUGGESTS, I consider myself the funniest man on the planet. In judging for yourself, you may wish to consider that humor of my type is often the product of some uncontrolled personality defect. This shouldn't matter when the result is so entertaining, and I have earned the title I propose on at least two occasions.

I went to the High School of Music and Art in Harlem, housed in a beautiful, venerable building that had stood witness to the early training of a hundred famous musicians in its lifetime. While I had been accepted to the school based upon my supposed proficiency on the piano and clarinet, my real talents lay elsewhere. This was demonstrated during the annual *Mother Ranking Contest,* an event perfectly suited to a group of sixteen-year-old boys.

For those who don't get the *lingo,* this was a competition where the funniest boys in the school (and therefore in the entire city, didn't you know?) took turns making defamatory and vulgar comments about each others' mothers. The whole thing was rather straightforward. It was held at lunchtime, in the cafeteria. Each pair of contestants squared off, one by one and one against the other, exchanging their toxic barbs. The winner was decided conclusively in this way: You had to make Jeff laugh.

Jeff was a big kid and my friend and a brown belt in Karate. He had a discriminating sense of humor – it was either funny to him or it wasn't – and it had to be *really* funny to make him laugh. Typically, any attempt at humor was more likely to produce a frown and a denigration of the attempted joke-teller. One by one, the participants would face him and sound off. One by one, he would brutally eliminate one or the other. Until only two of us remained, and one of those was me.

I knew the dude I was facing, and he was funny. He was

actually *really* funny, and crazy to boot, and he had this *black thing* going for him that I couldn't come close to emulating. This was going to be tough.

The rules for the final round were a bit different: you had to do more than just make Jeff laugh. You had to make him laugh *so* hard that milk would spill from his nose. The person who could accomplish this won the contest. The final round would continue until someone did.

As I've said, it was all rather straightforward. There was quite a crowd assembled. Everyone knew the stakes, and Jeff understood his role in all of this. He slowly, almost reverently picked up a fresh, half-pint container of milk. He pried open the top and inserted a short plastic straw in the V-shaped opening he had created.

He began to sip in steady and measured fashion – not too much and not too little – like a wine connoisseur savoring a fine Cabernet.

I can't recall what joke I told that won me the day and that opened up the *flood-milks* from Jeffrey's nostrils, or the degree of laughter that ensued. I do remember a fine white spray covering a dozen people, many of whom fell from their chairs in laughter or retreated in a mad dash to avoid it.

Such is the fabric from which the washcloths of our victories are woven.

I'm proud to add that the same happy result concluded our annual Spitball Contest and the rules were the same. If you could cover your opponent with enough spitballs to make Jeff laugh, you won. The final round...well, you know.

In every high school in America at that time, and in every high school in every civilized nation on earth, I imagine, there were the same plain white straws, in the same plain white paper wrappers. For reasons known only to chemists and other scientists, the paper that covered these plastic beauties, when combined with saliva, made stalwart projectiles that could be shot through the straw with a short puff of breath, and that could travel some distance. They also had the advantage of sticking to the object they struck, regardless of what it was, and functioned kind of like nature's crazy glue.

Some spitballers preferred to bite off pieces of the wrapper, forming the spitball in their mouths, a kind of rapid-fire approach to the whole thing. Others, like me, preferred the slower, but surer method of ripping off a piece of wrapper with their fingers, rolling it into a tight ball, and then popping it in their mouths for firing. However, this method often allowed your opponent to get a jump on you, and there was a chance you could be covered in spitballs before you had a chance to shoot.

I prepared for this eventuality the afternoon before the contest. A trip to the grocery store yielded an entire box of the straws used in school. Another trip to the candy store yielded an extra wide plastic straw that promised to perform the equivalent function of a machine gun. I returned home, sat on my bed, removed each wrapper from each straw in the box, and began to roll spitballs. I pressed down hard on each ball I rolled in order to achieve maximum density and killing power. I rolled over a hundred of them, I think, and placed them into an oversized pillbox.

I stepped into the cafeteria that day with the swagger of a gunfighter who knows he is the fastest gun in the west. No one had ever thought of this type of *preparation aforethought*; it wasn't *in* the (unwritten) rules, and it wasn't *not* in them.

Throughout the contest, I sparingly dipped into my reserve ammunition, and quickly realized that I had an advantage over every opponent who had to form his spitballs by either hand or mouth. Once again, I found myself in the final round and up against a good friend, Lonnie, who was not only a very funny guy himself, but a superb spitballer.

We faced off against each other with a deadly and quiet reserve. Jeff slowly sipped his milk and watched on with his full attention.

And, I waited. I waited, and I watched as Lonnie disassembled his first straw-wrapper, looking at me with mild curiosity, and wondering why I wasn't doing the same. My hand closed around the open pill bottle in my left pocket, which still contained half of my ammunition. From my right pocket, I removed my blunderbuss of a straw. I waited until Lonnie took his first bite of the wrapper and raised the straw to his lips with a look of eager anticipation and wistful mirth.

When he did, I poured the entire contents of the pill bottle into my mouth. In one smooth and fluid motion, I raised the straw to my lips. I blew with all my strength.

What I unleashed upon my good friend's face is no doubt still legend in that school. Projectiles were hurled at such blinding speed and in such volume from the customized straw that the audience gasped. Every one hit its intended target and Lonnie's face became covered with white dots, making him look as if he had been consumed by a fatal pox.

The milk erupted like a geyser from Jeffrey's face. He threw his chair back and choked, holding his throat, struggling for breath between his gasping cackles; milk all over him, all over the floor, and all over anyone within ten yards of him.

Well, I guess you had to be there. I don't know how many times we get to prove anything about ourselves or gain any recognition for some of our talents, however strange and obscure they may be. But *this* was *my* moment – OK, a stupid moment – but one reserved for me alone.

I add only this short anecdote…

I have given you, I pray, little reason to think that my comedy in any way diminished during my college years. In truth, it flourished, and some of you may tell me whether it is still flourishing today. However, I was not the only student enrolled in that vast edifice of knowledge that was Boston University who possessed comedic brilliance.

His name was Bruce, but we called him Fritz, and he was a solitary sort of guy. He was short and skinny, with a terminal case of *Alopecia*, which some of you might know as premature balding. The few tufts of hair that remained on his head made him look insane.

And, he was funny. Like me, he thought he was the funniest man on earth. Neither of us was shy about expressing our opinions or hesitated to prove our mastery of the art of comedy.

So, once a week, we would face off against each other. We'd sit on the floor of his dorm room and exchange barbs, each one funnier than the last, each of us gulping from a bottomless fountain of insults, gaffes, and vulgar tales. At the end of each session, we would each proclaim ourselves the funniest man on earth. But, in our hearts, I don't think either one of us was actually sure who was. Eventually, we would find out.

I graduated from BU one day, and Fritz disappeared off the face of the planet, becoming just one of a thousand fond memories I have of my college days. Until I saw him twenty years later.

He was not in a dorm room. He was on television. He was accepting an Emmy Award. He was a writer for Saturday Night Live.

Now *that's* funny.

A little part of me was jealous that day as I watched my old friend beaming on a TV screen, holding his award. But, mostly, I was grateful that he had been recognized for his brilliant wit.

Hell, if *he* was *that* funny, maybe I was, too.

What Happens In The Dorm *Stays* In The Dorm

OK, THIS TALE WILL BE JUST ABOUT AS RACY as anything you will find here. Of course, we had to have *one* story like this, didn't we? After all, at least some of you have racy stuff on your minds all the time, and this little book aims to please everyone.

Even people like *you*, that bald guy with the glasses in aisle 13.

If you're under 18, you shouldn't read this at all. Just skip over it and go on to the next chapter. There you'll find things like puppies, infants at play, and newborn tiger cubs.

On your honor, now.

We are back in Boston University, my third year of college, and I was at the height of my personal power. I no longer carried with me the naiveté of *freshman-ness*. I had not yet assumed the soon-to-be-dead-and-gone mantle that floated silently above the heads of all seniors. I was in the sweet spot of my college experience.

I was also feeling my oats, as they say, and diligently dedicating myself to my undeclared major and minor studies: partying my brains out and looking for girls.

But of *all* the girls at Boston University, there was this *one* girl; this gorgeous, beautiful, unreachable girl. I chatted with her every other day in class. I stood on the tiny balcony of my dorm room each morning waiting for her to walk by. She would always look up, wave and smile.

Her name was Susan, but she had a Farah Fawcett smile and long black hair that always seemed to be blowing back from her head as if an invisible wind machine was suspended in front of her as she walked. She had long, lean legs, always poured into skintight jeans, and the rest...well, the rest...*Whew*.

Anyway, the rumor was that she liked me, and most everyone knew I liked her. It seemed we just couldn't bridge the gap from friend-stage to anything more, probably a result of my shyness as much as anything else.

But I have found – through unnecessarily broad experience – that alcohol has a way of both bridging gaps and overcoming shyness, sometimes with unexpected results.

Put all this aside for a moment. But keep it in mind.

Now, I had these two other friends in college – Clark and Jay – and it's about time I introduced them to you. Clark was a monster of a man, six-foot-something and well over two hundred fifty pounds, with hands the size of a gorilla and wild brown hair that made him look quite mad. He was the former center of his high school football team. He tended to be reclusive and could be rather ill-tempered when crossed.

He was also my roommate and we developed a close bond with each other, like a Mutt and a Jeff. I functioned as his reasonable side and he operated as my brutal side. In practice, this meant that I spent a good amount of time trying to convince him not to injure people. He spent his time convincing people, in his unique way, that it would be foolish to try to injure me. It was a great friendship.

Jay, on the other hand, while possessing a personality similar to Clark's, tended to be less subtle. He was a kid from Portland, Maine. He always wore a flannel shirt, even in the summer. He had a curly red "Afro" and glasses that made him seem like a nerd. But he was anything but a nerd, because there was nothing Jay liked more than a good argument or a good fight. Or – better yet – a good argument leading to a good fight.

With beer, of course. Beer was the one thing we all had in common.

Anyway, the three of us were hanging out in my dorm room one day when we decided to visit Jay's friend, Tim. He lived in another dormitory; the infamous "700" building on Commonwealth Avenue. This three-towered fortress was the newest and most sterile living quarters on campus. My almost-girlfriend, Susan, lived in this dormitory, with her unbelievably hot roommate, Janet, a slim, perpetually dolled up blonde who you'd die to take home to Mommy. Or just take home. Keep this in mind, too.

Also living at 700 was a guy named Jack. He was the kind of handsome, spoiled, stuck-up rich kid who everyone hated, unless you were just like him. Everyone has had a Jack in their lives. Jack happened to live on the same floor as Tim.

Let me add this for those readers who may happen to be a bit like Jack themselves; the Jack I'm talking about was probably a good person deep inside. OK, *really* deep inside. Nevertheless, I am confident he grew into a productive and successful citizen. Perhaps he even became a hedge fund manager. I'm sure he possesses a fine moral grounding – or at least, that he enjoys a healthy confusion with respect to what is decent and what is not – and probably, has his own deeply conflicting version of the following events.

The three of us went to 700, had our laughs with Tim for a few hours, then left together as a trio, passing Jack's room on the way out. When Jack happened to open his door.

As I've intimated, we all knew Jack and we all disliked him in varying degrees. Jay's distaste was a bit more venal, however, and he couldn't pass up the opportunity – provided to him by a kind and benevolent fate – to remind Jack of this. This reminiscing took the form of fifteen minutes of spontaneous diatribe composed in various measure of four-letter expletives, humiliating descriptions of Jack's relations with farm animals, and charming anecdotes pertaining to his inability to have sex with a woman.

Jack did the only reasonable thing, I thought, and slammed the door in our faces. We all laughed, quite satisfied with the result, and that should have been the end of the matter.

But, it wasn't.

It occurs to me that some of you may be unfamiliar with

telephones that have long, pigtail-like cords extending from them and that connect to handsets you speak into and hear out of. Let me assure you that at one time these contraptions were quite the rage. In fact, at *that* time, *everyone* had one, and Jack had one mounted on the wall just by the door. When he slammed it shut, a loop of the cord got stuck in the door and protruded from it.

This was just too much temptation for Jay, who, with little hesitation, produced a knife from his pocket and gleefully slashed it. He allowed himself a moment to admire his work, and then, obviously delighted with the result, went back to Tim's room to share the news of his spectacular achievement. Clark trotted the other way towards the elevators. I was left somewhat rooted to the spot, staring at the severed cord, and rather dumbfounded at this unexpected turn of events. When Jack opened the door again.

We stared at each other. As riveting as his gaze was, I soon noticed he was holding half of his telephone cord in his hands. The receiver-end trailed from the wire and brushed the floor. Jack had a look of disbelief painted across his face. For a second I thought he was holding the tail of a dead possum, with its body dangling gruesomely on the floor. *That* would have been pretty *disbelievable*.

He looked at me. He looked down at the dead possum. He looked back at me and his look hardened. He *knew* that I had cut the cord. He *knew* this because the cord was cut and I was the only one there. For once, I was quite speechless.

Then Jack did something he really shouldn't have; he threatened me. Then, he threatened me again.

I mean, this guy was really a wimp, but he was an *angry* wimp right now. He did have good cause to be mad and I truly under-stood that the circumstances demanded that he focus his irritation upon me. Besides, I was a little guy, and he was bigger than a little guy. This had always made it much easier for people to be angry with me.

It was then that Clark poked his head around the corner of the hallway. He asked me a simple, straightforward question.

"Is he bothering you, Dave?"

"No, Clark, he's not bothering me at all," I dutifully responded, suddenly quite concerned. For Jack.

"I think he's bothering you, Dave," Clark replied.

"No, Clark, he isn't."

"I disagree, Dave."

With that, Clark charged around the corner, as mad bulls or high school centers are often wont to do. The mere sight of him was enough to drive Jack back into his room.

I am pleased to note that my gentle urgings to Clark convinced him to spare the poor boy's life. Had Jack only stopped whining and yapping when he should have, Clark wouldn't have taken the gloves he held in his hand and slapped him across the face, hard enough to propel him across the room and make his head look like one of those bobble-head dog *thingies* mounted on car dashboards.

And, still, *that* would have been the end of the matter, had Jack not reported the entire incident to the authorities, the authorities being the administration of Boston University.

For reasons not entirely understood by me, even to this day, only I was called before the dean. There was no mention of Clark's assault – possibly because Jack wisely feared another quite like it, only worse – and only the issue of the telephone cord was the apparent concern.

The incident was described to me. This was unnecessary as I had been there; I had seen the whole thing. I denied any culpability.

"If not you, then who?" the dean asked.

"Some kids I was with," I replied quite truthfully.

"Who?"

Now, this was just too much. I'd watched enough mob movies and had enough Italian friends to know a little about *Omerta*, the

Mafia's code of honor, which forbids the betrayal of either your friends or your enemies to any organized authority. Hell, I was from the *Bronx*. We had our *own* friggin' *Omerta*. So I decided not to squeal. My friends would have done the same for me, and I knew it, so I took the fall.

The fall was hard by any reasonable standards. I was put on probation for one year for something I didn't do and banned from the 700 dormitory for six months.

And *that surely* would have been the end of the matter, had I not gotten really, really wasted and really, really horny one Saturday night.

One of my snapshots puts me in a hallway, and on a phone located in that hallway at about 10 p.m. And, ladies and gentlemen, I was buzzed, really buzzed. With the reckless bravado and false courage that only a *buzzy* state of mind can produce, I decided to call my almost-woman, Susan, and tell her what I thought of her. In each successive thought, she was wearing fewer and fewer clothes.

I called. Janet picked up. I asked her where Susan was.

"Out," she replied.

A brilliant thought occurred to me as the image of Janet filtered through my mind.

"Well, what are *you* doing?" I inquired in my very best oh-so-innocent voice.

"Nothing at all," she replied, which I thought a very proper response, indeed.

"Why don't I come over then?"

"That would be nice," she said.

All men are dogs, as my wife is fond of saying and, in many ways, I think, correctly. She's also fond of saying that when it comes to men, the little head often speaks for the big one. This, too, I think is true.

Trust me when I say that the little head was the only head that I was listening to. I headed for the 700 dormitory.

I was *banned*, you say? Well, of course I was! But that's what the *big* head was saying! In a very, very quiet little voice. While the idea of Janet had never entered either of my heads before, it was sure driving nails right then and there. In fact, it was driving all that silly talk of being banned right out of my head; one of them or the other, or both for all I know. So, I prepared.

You see, to get into 700 in those days, you had to scale a towering escalator that led to a front desk that marked the entrance. At the entrance were two security guards. You could get in by showing a guard a pass demonstrating you had been invited by a resident and were cleared to enter. Since I passed through various dormitories most every week, I had a small supply of such passes. With a few clever alterations – a date changed here, a name changed there – I had my ticket to ride.

Get to the desk; flash the pass; walk by as if nothing is happening.

Well, that was the plan.

I got to the entrance, flashed my pass to one disinterested security guard, and took a step past the threshold of the entry. I was in. Piece of cake.

Except.

Except for the only thing I *hadn't* planned on; the one thing I couldn't *possibly* have anticipated. That at this late hour of a Saturday night, when any self-respecting rich kid would be out spending his daddy's money, Jack would be talking sports with the other security guard standing to the left of the entrance.

I felt the muscles in my face slacken. My jaw dropped. I looked at Jack, quite astonished. On his face, I saw a very similar expression of *flabber-gastedness*, but one that only lasted a moment.

"You!" he exclaimed.

"You?" I asked.

"You're banned from this dormitory!" he opined.

"Am I?" I inquisitively replied.

"You are!" he insisted.

I smiled. Then, I ran.

What followed would have made the Keystone Kops proud. Jack screamed and pointed at me wildly, as if he'd just spotted John Dillinger himself or as if I had busted out of some medical quarantine and was about to spread a particularly virulent strain of the Ebola virus to the student body. As the security guards leaped into action, I just leaped. What followed was a short-lived, but highly comical chase around couches and pillars which commanded the attention of the dozens of students milling around the lobby.

"Rent-a-cops!" I muttered angrily under my breath as I bobbed and weaved.

"Pigs!" I added, with a guttural and bitter satisfaction (hey, it was the '70s) as I ducked and darted to and fro.

Finally, with a small burst of speed fueled by no small burst of adrenaline, I blurred past one rather obese and heavy-breathing rent-a-whatever, who clearly lacked the ability to capture such a wily and dangerous fugitive. I burst through the door of the "B" tower staircase, scurried up three flights in a lightning flash, exploded through the staircase door, traversed the length of the hall, entered the rear staircase, flew down one flight and stopped, panting and sweating, on the second floor.

Friggin' Jack, I thought, shaking my head in rank disbelief at the rare and exquisite quality of my hard luck.

Each of the three towers that comprised this dormitory had its own elevator bank and staircases, which all connected to the lobby. In other words, no one tower was accessible to any other, except from the lobby. I needed to get to "C" tower, where Janet was, but I had to go through the lobby to do it, and in doing so, pass right by the guard station.

Being in B tower, however, was a good place to construct a Plan B, and I did so rapidly. While I couldn't reach the C tower from where I was, I could simply hang out for a while. I could wait for the heat to die down and the coast to clear, and then nonchalantly stroll through the lobby with a small group of students as cover and make my way to the dame.

This had been a lot more work and effort than I'd planned on, but hey, everything could still work out OK. After all, there was a pot of gold at the end of the rainbow.

Or more accurately, a room full of Janet at the end of the hallway.

I waited twenty minutes, long enough for any college security guard's short-term memory to fail him and long enough to compel him in the direction of more deadly and pervasive perils. Say, a loose lid on a coffee cup or a pen running out of ink.

I returned to the lobby level, opened the heavy steel door of the staircase an inch and peered through the slit. The lobby seemed quiet and mostly deserted. Not a creature was stirring, not even a pig or a mouse. Encouraged, I quietly slipped out, put on my best "who, me?" face, and casually strolled to the C tower elevator bank no more than fifty feet away.

I got halfway there, too. That was when I noticed Jack was still waiting by the entrance, with his two uniformed friends.

There was no escaping them this time, and this time I didn't try, at least not right away. The guards seized me simultaneously, each lifting me by one arm, and in this manner began to escort me to the entrance, with my feet hanging in the air. Truth be told, I was quite exhausted by then and at first the sensation of traveling without physical effort was quite relaxing. Then, I started to think. "What are they going to do with me?" I asked myself. "Are they going to throw me out?"

"Well, *of course* they are!" my big head cried.

"*What about Janet!*" screamed my little head, clearly not appreciating the gravity of our situation at all.

The intentions of the rabid guards were becoming less clear by the moment.

Perhaps they were going to "detain" me. Could they do that?

Would they lock me in a room? Would they Scotch Tape me to a bunk bed?

I realized that I was probably panicking unduly. I calmed myself and focused on the more likely prospect that the guards would simply report me to the administration.

Or maybe they would just call the police! Was I going to be arrested? Could you get arrested for something like this?

Obviously my big head had already decided that this was not a time for being calm and my little head probably wouldn't have permitted it anyway. I didn't know the answer to any of my questions, but I did know I wasn't going to wait there with my newfound goon buddies to find out the answers.

The second I saw an opportunity, I twisted out of the grip of both guards, crashed through the entrance and leaped the wrong way down an escalator, fairly flying over the tops of the treads, past startled students and down, down, down into the clean night air and freedom.

I was winded and shaken when I hit the streets, but I was free, at least for the moment.

"What about Janet!" my little head pleaded again.

While I found this pitiful display of single-minded self-indulgence quite disappointing, it was clear that my little head was disgusted by the clumsiness of my efforts throughout the entire affair.

I called Janet, mostly just to shut it up. I explained the situation to her. She listened quite politely. She was sympathetic, but somewhat taken aback.

I understood her reaction. After all, there was no way I could have expected her to know of my notorious and dodgy nature.

I asked whether she would consider meeting me downstairs. Her response is as clear in my mind now as it was to my ears then.

"I can't," she said.

"Why not?" I asked.

"Because I don't have any clothes on," she replied.

I will let your imaginations do the rest, dear readers; there will be no snappy comebacks here, and no storybook endings, either.

Our Maine Mistake

MY DEAR COLLEGE BUDDY, JAY, one of the stars of the previous tale, is from Maine. Looked at from the vantage point of a Northern Canadian seeking to escape the cold winter weather, Maine is probably a balmy getaway. But, for anyone else, it's a very, very cold place, and it's particularly cold in the mountains of Maine on December 31st of any given year. That's where Jay and I were headed way back when, to a New Year's Eve party, somewhere high on a mountain peak in that beautiful state.

Let me emphasize that the party was going to be somewhere on the very *top* of a mountain. I don't know why this was so, or why anybody would think of constructing anything at all in such a place other than an igloo, a weather observatory tower, or an Arctic-like research station where stranded scientists are forced to contend with murderous aliens.

Anyway, it was a party, and it was a *New Year's Eve* party. I had never been to Maine, but Jay had lived there all his life. He knew his way around.

Of course he did. That was why, at the beginning of our journey, when his car began to run out of gas and he pulled into a station, I never thought of questioning his decision to purchase only two dollars' worth.

It's true that gasoline was under a dollar a gallon then. No, we weren't driving a Model T, but let me assure you that even then, two dollars was not a lot of gas to put in an empty tank when you were going on an extended drive.

I did look at him strangely, of course, because even at the age of nineteen I had an iota of common sense. But it was a very small iota.

But, hey: Jay had lived in Maine all his life. He knew his way around. Didn't he?

Of course he did. So we set off.

It was a beautiful drive and a beautiful day for a drive as we cut our way through majestic pines on curving mountain roads in the clear, clean, crisp, invigorating, *friggin' freezing* mountain air.

And it was a nice party; it really was. At some point – I don't exactly remember when – I realized that I was in a hotel. At some point thereafter, I realized that most of the partygoers were staying at the hotel and had no cause whatever to drive back down the mountain afterward.

Well, *all* of them were staying at the hotel, actually, except us. We left around one in the morning, and we got a few miles, too; halfway down, I'd say. Then, Jay – always the responsible driver – checked his gas gauge and announced we were running out of gas.

Reality check: There were no gas stations. There were no cell phones. There were no other cars on the road. There wasn't even an Arctic research station in sight. We were doomed.

I glared at him in incriminating fashion.

As I've previously suggested, Jay loved to argue, and he loved to fight, and everything he said or did was usually designed to provoke one or the other. He glared back at me and flashed his teeth in a snarl as if he blamed *me* for our predicament, fairly daring me to say, "I told you so," or "what an idiot you are," or something like that.

Which, I did not, because Jay was the craziest person I knew. I had observed him put his fist through a plate glass window, and brawl with a guy 100 pounds heavier. I thought it best to just keep silent and let the cold kill me slowly. I guess I preferred a *demise-deferred* rather than one that might result without any delay at all.

He pulled over to the side of a wilderness road on a night as dark and as cold as any I've ever seen or experienced. *I* thought we should have continued to drive until we *actually* ran out of gas. At least we would have been *attempting* to survive. Besides, who knew what miracles might transpire when a desperate prayer was combined with the fumes remaining in a gas tank?

But *Jay* felt we should just pull over and give up. *Jay* thought our *strandedness* was a *fait accompli*. Perhaps he felt it simply wasn't worth the effort. To survive.

OK.

We left the engine running for as long as the gas lasted, and it didn't last long. We settled in for our last, long, frigid night on the planet, Jay in the back seat and me in the front. It was cold.

I'm confident that many of you already know that the word "cold" has a different meaning in northeastern states like Maine, Vermont, and New Hampshire. I'm not schooled in the physics of all this, but I do know that in such places the cold pierces your skin like a knife. No normal piece of clothing seems sufficient to keep it at bay for long.

As well, most Americans, and most people anywhere, understand that regardless of their own *polarbearability*, that thirty degrees is *pretty cold*, that fifteen degrees is *much* colder, and that five degrees is *really, really* cold.

So, everyone can understand that seven degrees below zero is much colder than that – because that was the overnight temperature where we were stranded.

It's probably true that young people everywhere are totally convinced – without needing to even consider the issue – that they will live forever. They believe that they're invulnerable to just about anything, including their foolish recklessness and deadly sub-zero temperatures. I was no exception, and while I admit that the thought of dying did not occur to me, the thought of suffering certainly did. Huddled in a fetal ball on the front seat, shivering, chilled to the bone although it was only 2 a.m., through chattering teeth I said, "…God, Jay, it's cold."

"I know," he confirmed.

Then, my inner Gremlin contributed its two cents, as it has often done so generously throughout my life, said two cents taking the form of a subtle, three-word suggestion more valuable than a two-penny. Here is what the Gremlin said:

"Look at Jay."

Having nothing else to do but suffer, freeze, pass out and ultimately expire, I felt I had nothing to lose by following up upon its suggestion. I turned my head towards the back seat for a peek at Jay.

An old family legend crossed my mind. It was the story of my dad, a decorated veteran of World War II, who flew in a B-24 Liberator Bomber. In those days, there was no heat in the planes, and the crew was kept alive by multiple electric heating units located throughout their flight suits. On one flight, the heating unit in the pilot's boot malfunctioned. It wouldn't take long for frostbite to set in, and by the time the plane landed, the foot would be lost to the deep cold of thirty thousand feet.

Thinking quickly, my father told the pilot to remove his boot. Dad opened his jacket and kept the pilot's foot under his arm for the remainder of the flight, providing the warmth necessary to prevent frostbite and amputation, and earning himself a medal in the process.

Maybe my dear friend was blue in the lips. Could he have stopped breathing? Perhaps he had stopped breathing and his life was in danger. I was, after all, my father's son. Perhaps it was hero time.

Not. Not when I looked back and saw Jay comfortably curled up under a huge woolen blanket.

Using a number of colorful, highly descriptive words, I told my friend how delighted I was that he was safe and warm. I acknowledged his laudable efforts to ensure that at least one of us survived the disaster he had created. I persuaded him to join me in the front seat, where we huddled miserably under the blanket, barely sleeping until daybreak.

We awoke on the first day of the New Year to find ourselves still stranded and still frozen. We were surrounded by glorious pines, gorgeous cliffs, and snow so white it hurt your eyes to look at it, on as beautiful and sunny a winter day as could be found anywhere.

There was not another living thing in sight. There was little question that the heat generated by the entire State of Maine did not amount to that produced by a single matchstick ignited underwater.

We turned on the radio. We learned it had warmed to zero degrees. This was uplifting, as it demonstrated that our fortunes were improving.

I stepped out of the car and looked down the road to the left, then to the right.

Nothing. We waited. And waited.

About an hour later a car appeared up the road. I stood by the side of the road and waved, fully aware of the reputation of Mainers for neighborliness, and confident the driver would realize our predicament and be glad to lend a hand.

Not really. I still had a few happy thoughts like this remaining when the third car passed us by two hours later, but not that many. I realized it was just as easy to be murdered by the weather in the daylight as it was during the evening hours. Then, I got this idea.

I got this idea that I had to convince someone to stop. More accurately, I had to *make* someone stop. The only thing I could think of was to start a fire, but not to alert a passerby to our emergency. My intention was to erect a flaming barrier across the road. This might prove a lot more convincing than a friendly wave, or even a skirt hiked high above an extended leg.

Crazy you say? OK, but understand I didn't have a lot of options.

But I did have a lighter.

I started to gather tree branches from the side of the road. I checked my pocket for my lighter, not thinking all this through, exactly, except to note to myself that desperate times required desperate measures.

I am pleased to report that a roadside blaze was not necessary. Sometime during the third hour a pickup cruised down the road.

"My fire isn't ready!" I silently screamed to myself, knowing that the truck would pass us by in seconds. Clearly desperate, I did the only thing that a person genetically disposed to acts of heroism could do under the circumstances.

I walked to the center of the road, blocked the car's path, and closed my eyes.

If I represent to you that this tale has not been written by any of my heirs or beneficiaries, you can probably guess how it ends, which is in a gay and happy fashion, like most everything you have read here. We were picked up by a gentlemanly, if somewhat startled driver and deposited some miles away in a sleepy little mountain town where nothing but the local diner was open. *Nothing* but the diner; including the town's one gas station.

It was New Year's Day. Did I mention that? Oh, I did.

In any event, I can feel that first blast of heat from the restaurant's interior as viscerally today as I did then, and it was a pleasant *viscerality* indeed. I ordered steak and eggs; a meal ideally suited for cowboys, Arctic researchers, and stranded travelers.

It was the best meal I've ever had. Fortunately for us, the sole proprietor of the town's lone gas station did decide to open after all, but after breakfast time, and for only one pair of customers. He not only lent us a gas can, but drove us back to our stranded vehicle.

In the can was two dollars' worth of gasoline. It was a stark reminder of our foolishness, and of an old Boy Scout saying.

Something about proper preparation, I think.

Nothing Magic About This Mountain

MY FEAR OF ROLLER COASTERS is legendary in my family, but I assure you that I possess a *courageous* kind of fear in this regard. Let me explain.

It started when I was about eight and Dad took me on a roller coaster in Coney Island's famous Astroland Park. It wasn't really a roller coaster, it was more like a giant bug that ran around in circles, and it was named after one.

"The Caterpillar" was a long, tubular ride that traversed a bumpy course that followed a rough oval. Halfway through the ride a green canopy would enclose the revelers – typically delighted children and their parents – making the ride look just like its namesake. It was still a *kiddie ride,* you understand. It had no steep drops, it didn't turn you upside down or go around in circles at the speed of light, or use centrifugal force to hold the tiny bodies of vulnerable children in place while they screamed.

It didn't go all that fast, either, at least not by the standards of today's modern contraptions, where merely exceeding the speed of sound is for *girlie-girls* and *Mach Five* is not only a possibility, but a requirement.

But, it was *much* faster than I could tolerate at that age, (and more than I could bear fifty years later) so I did what any self-respecting child would do when faced with such unpleasantness: I screamed.

Of course, many people scream on roller coasters, but their shrieks are typically expressions of delight, not terror. My scream was of a somewhat different tenor. I seem to remember it began moments before the green canvas of the ride rose around me, and reached a certain peak when I was sealed in completely, leaving nothing but shadows inside as the ride convulsed up, down and around.

Mine was a wail of *abject* terror, the result of a horror so unspeakable that it would be more easily associated with slow mutilation than with a carnival ride for small children.

I guess every carny in America hears a million yelps, squeals, screeches and screams in his lifetime. Maybe, carnies can't even sleep at night if someone isn't screaming in the background. When someone screams, maybe a carny thinks he's being paid a compliment, as if someone's saying, "Hey, you scared the crap out of me! Thanks!"

But *this* scream stood out among all the screams the man operating the Caterpillar had ever heard. He stopped the ride immediately and I was lifted out, weeping and shuddering.

Twenty *roller-coasterless* years passed. And then came Disneyworld.

For anyone who lived on the East Coast, California's Disney*land* was a million miles away. But when Disney*world* came to Florida, everything changed, making all of that California magic suddenly accessible. And with Disneyworld came Magic Mountain.

My brother and I found ourselves in the park when we were in our late twenties. I should also mention that Matthew shares none of my roller coaster-related disabilities.

The ride truly looked magnificent. This was unlike any roller coaster I'd ever seen, mostly because it didn't look anything like a roller coaster. It was just this huge structure, dressed up to look like a mountain. Park-goers were expected to blithely walk through a hole in the mountain to enter the ride. I found this both funny and frightening all at the same time.

I had to admit this thing looked *cool*. I mean, it was outrageous and exotic and one of a kind. This wasn't just a ride, this was an *experience*, and I considered whether this was an experience I wanted to miss. But, only for a moment. This was a damn *roller coaster*. What was I thinking?

As we stood from afar and sized up the ride, my brother kindly sensed my concerns. He wanted to help, he really did.

"Let me go up there and see how fast it is," he offered.

"OK," I replied.

I watched as he strolled to the entrance and conversed with a security guard. They had an animated conversation. It all ended with Matt energetically nodding his head up and down and vigorously shaking the man's hand in thanks. He returned.

My good-hearted brother nodded his head to me as he approached. He extended his right arm around my shoulder and pointed to the entrance of the ride. He explained what the guard had said to him, namely, that there was a "fast side" and a "slow side" to this attraction. Patrons could choose how fast they wished to go as they rushed headlong down the artificial slopes of this mountain's peaks.

Indeed, as my eyes followed my brother's gesture, I noticed that there was not one, but two holes in the artificial mountainside, and that two lines of people had formed, one at each hole. I was a bit suspicious, but I was also encouraged and cautiously made my way towards the "slow" entrance, with my brother urging (well, *pulling*) me along.

We slowly advanced up a very, very long and very, very dark circular ramp that seemed to stretch on forever. Every twenty feet or so, a sign was posted along the ramp. Its headline was in red, bold, capital letters, and its message was pretty clear: *CAUTION*. It listed forty or so medical conditions. Apparently, if you had one of these, you should consider taking another ride, perhaps the one with little teacups that go round and round for a bit. I considered myself a relatively healthy person but pointed out to my sibling that I had three of the listed ailments.

He laughed. He urged me not to worry. After all, was I a man or a mouse? A mere roller coaster couldn't kill anyone unless you took your restraints off in the middle of the ride and leaped off. *No one* would do *that*. *Everybody* had at least one or two of the medical conditions listed on the sign. The sign was just erected at the advice of lawyers, anyway, and *they* had probably never even *seen* this ride.

You get the idea.

As I walked up the never-ending ramp, I heard blood-curdling screams in the distance, like walking into your home and hearing a slasher movie blasting from the television in the next room.

Finally, we reached the end of the ramp and the top of the mountain, so to speak, and the ramp emptied into a large chamber. As it did, I stopped cold. And, I saw.

What I saw was a group of people entering from the far side of the expansive area. It took me only a second or two to realize that what I was witnessing was the *second* line of people I had observed. These people had lined up for the "fast side" of the ride. Both lines – the fast and the *less-than-fast* lines – emptied into this common area.

In other words, both lines led to the same place. In other words, there was no distinction between the two lines.

In other words, there was no "slow" side. In other words, I had been snookered.

I didn't have to look at Matt to realize that he was waiting for this epiphany to burst into my brain. His uncontrolled hysterics – accompanied by what appeared to be severe stomach cramps and fits of weeping, as memorable as they were – did little to reduce the panic rising in my gut, or the alarming increase in my blood pressure, which seemed to actually force air out of my ears like the smokestack of a locomotive belches smoke and steam.

Except for the entrances, there appeared to be no other possible exits, other than two, huge, cylinder-shaped holes in one wall, each containing a blackness stolen from the darkest of nights. Before each hole was a group of four attendants, and before each group rested the result of a mating between a rocket ship and a giant vitamin capsule. The attendants feverishly labored to secure people into these things, reminding me of those guys who change the tires for race car drivers. When they secured the passengers, the giant vitamin lurched a few yards forward and simply dropped down the throat of the rabbit hole before it.

I looked at the two entrances again and imagined myself pushing past all those people for three hours while I attempted a pitiful retreat accompanied by the jeers and guffaws of those disgusted by my cowardice. That wasn't going to work. It was one thing to be spineless, but quite another to publicly advertise it. There was only one way out.

My brother comforted me in mocking fashion. I smiled. He had no idea what I was going to do to him if I survived, and that pleasant thought actually did comfort me. So, together, we stepped into the waiting *whatever-it-was*.

I soon saw why there were so many attendants. Two would work in tandem on one passenger. Together, they pulled down metal bars, tightened leather straps, and affixed various plastic restraints.

As I sat down in the capsule, I had three simultaneous reveries. First, I mused that this was like opening day at a new bondage club. Second, I imagined I was being tied to a hospital gurney, compelled to undergo an involuntary surgical sterilization. Finally, I thought of three black and white movies, all where a guy was strapped to an electric chair. James Cagney might have been in all of them.

I considered these scenarios carefully and viewed all three somewhat favorably compared to my current circumstance. With that, I found myself bolted into the rocket, and soon disappeared down the rabbit hole myself.

That the ride was memorable I concede. Thankfully, there were no sudden, sanity-bursting drops in altitude, but those things did reach speeds of about a zillion miles an hour. With every turn, I felt like I was tethered to a race car whose driver had just popped the clutch and floored it. A fascinating light show, composed principally of blurs, followed us all the way down, accompanied by the music of screeches, squeals, and shrieks.

Of course, it wasn't until the end of the ride that I realized that I had been the composer of that happy chorus and that the screams I had heard ringing in my ears were none other than my own.

Women Scare Me When They Don't Notice You're Dead

MY WIFE'S PERSONALITY is quite distinct from my own, and this is a good thing. After all, we don't want our wives to be *like* us, do we? No, of course we don't. We want them to *compliment* us, providing those sterling attributes which we lack. We wish them to possess that reliable judgment, that down-to-earth, good old-fashioned American common sense that might one day preserve our families or our fortunes, or our lives. Right?

Right. So, let it not be said that I am suggesting my wife has poor judgment. Poor eyesight, perhaps, but not poor judgment.

This isn't really the point I wish to make. The point I wish to make is that there's a slight statistical possibility she wants me dead.

Perhaps I should clarify.

I have to go back to 1987, two years before I would make Andrea my bride, when our love was fresh, and emerging, and new. It was a wonderful time.

I worked as an administrator for a private school in Queens, housed in a newly-renovated three-storey tenancy. It was a Friday, and it was July, and it was 95 degrees outside, and I was meeting my bride-to-be for dinner after work. She arrived around 5:45 in the afternoon – pretty as a picture – and sat down quite demurely in the lobby to wait for me. By 6 o'clock, all the staff had gone home. I emerged from my office, greeted my dearest, and told her we could leave the moment I locked the classroom doors on the third floor.

"Be just a minute!" I promised.

Always easy-going and agreeable, Andrea nodded pleasantly and ripped a book from her purse. She would be happy to linger for me, she said.

What a sweetheart, I thought. And with that pleasant thought in mind, I trotted off to the elevator just a few yards away.

The elevator had neatly escaped the renovation of the building. It was the original machine installed in the structure seventy years earlier and it was little more than a rickety antique. It was reliably *unreliable* and its operation was known to produce a genuine jolt of fear every now and again, and I knew this.

But I was only going to the third floor. I mean, what could happen?

I have previously written of Gremlins that reside in all of us, little beasts that often present themselves as a nagging sense of *something* tickling the back of our brains. As I paused before the elevator, one of my Gremlins gently tugged at me. This one was typically inclined to communicate in three-word phrases, and offered one such phrase on this occasion.

"Consider the stairs."

Like any skilled manager, I was always interested in the opinions of those working with me, or even *in* me, even if those opinions contrasted with my own. I seriously considered the urgings of the sprite that had whispered into my ear; I really did.

Then, I pressed the button to the elevator. The doors slowly parted with a groan. I stepped in and pressed the button for the third floor. The doors closed behind me with some finality, and the elevator rose in excruciatingly sluggish fashion.

I looked around me, taking a moment to admire the decorative, gold-painted ironwork that was the elevator's interior. As the compartment began to climb, I saw the square tube that contained it on all sides through the ironwork and the thick loops of rubber and steel cable that were lifted and lowered as the elevator rose.

There was no air conditioning in there, and it was like a hotbox. But I was only going to the third floor.

The elevator began to shudder and complain and appeared to slow as I passed the second floor. Then, it jerked. Then, it stopped.

I waited a moment. These things usually resolved themselves. This thing did not. I loosened my tie and unbuttoned the top button of my shirt. Gee, it was hot. I pressed the button to the second floor, then the button to the third floor. I repeated this procedure. Nothing.

I stood back and folded my arms across my chest. I reminded myself that I was a skilled manager whose ilk did not panic when presented with a complex dilemma, regardless of whether I had created the dilemma or not. I carefully studied the elevator's brass control panel. To its right was mounted a communications device; a small plastic mouthpiece that had been painted over to match the gold of the interior. Of course, there was no longer any cord attached to that mouthpiece, and no one to speak to had there been.

The panel itself contained a switch to turn off the elevator's interior light. (No!) Besides the floor numbers, there was only one other button; it was red and labeled *"Alarm."*

That would be the one. I pushed it.

What resulted was a sound like an old fire bell that stayed on as long as I held the button. After holding the button for a while, I began to push it over and over again in staccato fashion. Then, when I thought I had done *that* long enough, I sat down in the cabin and awaited my rescue.

After all, Andrea was "lingering" downstairs. I was only between the second and third floors and she must have heard the alarm. She would vault up the stairs, figure out that I was trapped in the elevator and do *something* to get me the hell out of there, even if it meant calling the fire department.

That was who you called, wasn't it?

Anyway, that's what I thought. My inner Gremlin was completely silent, perhaps shaking its head back and forth in unvoiced disapproval. More likely, it was giggling to itself hysterically with its hand plastered over its little Gremlin mouth.

I waited. I looked at my watch. Five minutes had passed since

I had sounded the alarm. I rose and began to press the alarm again, now in more urgent fashion, finally varying the tempo and pattern to include an SOS in Morse code.

I had seen this accomplished with great success in a movie once. In that film, a desperate sailor trapped in a submarine, tapped out the code onto a pipe using a metal wrench. I saw no reason whatever why this technique, having been so successfully executed in a sub on the silver screen, should not work just as well in an elevator shaft in real life.

Again, I sat on the floor and waited, staring at my watch as I did. Another five minutes passed as the sweat poured from my brow and dripped to the floor. I noticed the wafting of my own stink but considered that what I *might* be smelling was the charming aroma of me being *cooked*. After all, I had placed myself in an oven and seemed to have arrived in perfect time for the barbecue. This thought propelled me to my feet. I began to panic. I alternately pressed and *punched* the elevator buttons, yelling my almost-wife's name. I abruptly discontinued this foolishness when a thought occurred to me. I remembered that it was Friday.

"Friday…" I said out loud, to no one at all. "*After* Friday is…" I said aloud again.

After Friday was *the whole friggin' weekend*. Also, the length of time I might expect to be stuck in this box, which was now starting to feel very much like a coffin.

As I've stated, I started to panic. *Then*, I finished what I started. Let's just say that my performance included pulling my hair with both hands, while imploring the ceiling to do something.

This actually made sense at the time. Beyond the ceiling, I was sure, was a kind and benevolent God, who would hear my prayers. Andrea, for her part, was clearly hearing-impaired, and there appeared to be little sense attempting to communicate with her.

Somewhere in the middle of my screaming, begging, and self-flagellation, I noticed a steel plate about two feet square that looked like it was bolted to the ceiling of the compartment. I recognized it as an emergency escape hatch, undoubtedly placed there for people just like me. *Where* anyone might escape *to* eluded me. I looked around me to see if there was anything I had overlooked. I looked at my watch and realized I had left Andrea twenty minutes ago. Wouldn't she realize that something must have happened to me?

Of course she would.

Of course she would not. I was on my own. By the time she realized I wasn't returning (if she did); by the time she realized where I was (if she could); by the time help actually arrived (if they could break down the front door to the school, which I'd wisely secured, using a key currently in my possession); I would be...well, I suppose I would be either dead or disabled.

I searched my brain, trying to imagine another possible result. No – that was about it – dead or disabled. The Gremlin certainly had nothing else to offer, and I imagined it had already passed out from laughter.

The metal plate covering the escape hatch was about two feet above my head. I saw that it had one screw on either side that fastened it to the ceiling. I jumped the distance and struck the covering with my hand. It moved. The screws that once held it fast had failed some time ago; it wasn't secured at all and I was encouraged. I could escape!

I would climb out the hatchway and scramble to the top of the elevator. I would stand on the top of the car like the first man who had scaled Mount Everest. I would pound my chest in triumph like a gorilla and roar.

And then, soon thereafter, I would be either dead or disabled. But I didn't see what choice I had.

I leaped at the hatch with greater force, with both of my palms extended. They struck the sheet metal on target and the covering flew off, to where I could not fathom. I took a deep breath, crouched low and leaped again, with both of my hands finding the edge of the opening I had created. As I hung there, suspended, my feet reached for and found a thin brass rail located on the wall opposite the door of the car. With the rail as leverage, I thrust myself through the hole and to the top of the car.

The smell of burnt oil greeted me. I looked up and saw a small, but beautiful skylight rising to a delicate spire above me. I guessed that the car was designed to stop some distance from the skylight. Of course, it was only a guess. I was able to confirm that the car had come to rest between the second and third levels. The third-floor landing was at my eye level, and the door leading to the third floor was above my head.

I stood, like an idiot, on the top of the elevator. My shirt was dank with sweat and covered in grease, as were my pants, hands, and face. I was in a sauna, a sauna set too high and I still wasn't sure what I was going to do next. Without thinking, I leaped and grabbed the inner mechanisms of the exit door above me and pulled myself to the small, steel ledge at its bottom. As I hung there, holding on with my left hand, I started to fiddle with the various metal bars crisscrossing the door.

After I'd fiddled for some time, and after I'd achieved exactly nothing, I vaulted back to my perch on top of the elevator with an alarming *thud*, as the car beneath me shifted and complained.

I looked at the third-floor door closely. It *seemed* to be constructed to open manually from this side. That would have made sense, as someone must have installed the elevator's emergency hatch for a purpose. In other words, there *had* to be somewhere to *go* once you escaped the compartment. I reasoned that no elevator designer could have possibly had so gigantic a sense of humor as to omit an avenue of escape.

I was ready to try again when the elevator car lurched upward about a foot. Apparently, it hadn't abandoned its struggle to reach the third floor. While impressed by the machine's dedication and perseverance, I was wholly unimpressed by its common sense, as I was nearly thrown into the elevator shaft by the movement. As soon as I regained my balance it lurched again.

While this little jaunt had been interesting, it now seemed clear that I was located in what had become an exceedingly dangerous place. I looked up again. The skylight was maybe six feet away. If the elevator started moving, it would close that distance in seconds. If it decided to – and, who knew what facts an inanimate object might take into consideration before it did – my choice would be to either flatten myself against the top of the car and hope I wouldn't be crushed or leap blindly back into the car through the hatch, which was narrow enough to break both of my arms in the process.

These were terrible choices, but as stated, I was a skilled manager. I was perfectly capable of making complex decisions during periods of unusual stress, particularly when made necessary by my own unique brand of foolishness. I quickly decided to take the second option if the need arose and launched myself back on the ledge above for another try at the third-floor door.

The thought of returning to the car and allowing the elevator a bit more time to complete its journey did not occur to me.

Ultimately, I freed myself by violently operating a steel bar which released the door. I jumped through the opening into the relatively chilled air of the third floor. I wandered slowly down the hall, exhausted from my ordeal, and dragged myself down two flights of stairs and back to the lobby.

Where my wife-to-be was waiting, and where I'd left her one hour before: reading her book.

I approached her like one of the walking dead, and I certainly smelled the part, my hair wild about my head and my suit in grease-stained tatters. I halted before her, silently urging her to witness my physical state. She looked up and smiled. Then, she returned to her book.

"Ready to go?" she asked, still reading, and now somewhere around page 127.

I was incredulous. "Sweetheart, did you hear the alarm?" I asked.

"Yes, of course," she replied.

"Did you hear it ring a lot of times?"

"Yes, I did."

"Did you consider that I might be in some trouble and was trying to alert you?"

"No," she replied.

"May I ask why not?"

"I thought you were fooling around," she said, looking up and fluttering her eyelashes.

"You thought I was fooling around?" I asked. I merely wished her to repeat the words my brain told me she couldn't have possibly spoken.

"Yes; I thought you were fooling around," she confirmed.

At the time, it didn't occur to me that my new love wished me harm of any kind. That would be silly. This was a simple oversight on her part, a simple mistake of fact. She had no reason to believe that my life had been in danger.

Could have happened to anybody, I thought to myself.

So, I married her.

But, years later, something else happened.

I was afflicted with food poisoning, which I assure you feels exactly like it sounds. You're *poisoned*, you see, and said poisoning is accompanied by a broad variety of gastrointestinal symptoms of the most severe kind. I visited the bathroom for some time to wrestle with mostly *all* of these symptoms and, while I will omit the gory details of exactly what occurred there, suffice it to say that it was painful, and prolonged, and that my suffering was accompanied by a variety of barnyard noises over which I had little control.

I surfaced some time later; weak, faint and in obvious distress.

My wife was lying in bed, munching corn chips and reading a book with the television on. She had been in this exact position when I entered the bathroom one hour earlier. She did not remove her eyes from her book as I emerged.

There often seems to be a book involved when these things happen to me. I don't know why.

"How do you feel?" she asked, still reading as the TV boomed something about beets and apricots.

"Not so good," I replied as I crossed the path of the television, slowly struggling to get to my side of the bed.

While I was somewhere midway across the foot of the bed and directly in front of the TV, the world, and everything in it, went away.

When existence returned, my right cheek was pressed hard against the floor. I opened my eyes and realized with dim recognition that I was looking under my bed. Drool poured from my mouth and covered my lips and my chin, creating a small puddle on the floor, which my head had mistaken for a pillow.

I rose slowly and with great difficulty, my brain spinning. As I did, my eyes reached the edge of the bed and I saw my darling beloved. She was still lying there, munching on corn chips, reading her book. The TV was blaring something about mango salsa.

I stayed there for a moment, on my knees, and stared at her, now reeling with disbelief as well as dehydration. Her eyes did not shift a millimeter from her book.

"Sweetheart?" I asked, in as pleasant a tone as I could muster.

"Yes?" she inquired sweetly.

"Did you see me on the floor, darling?" I asked.

"Yes, I did," she said.

"How long was I down there?"

"For about five minutes."

"Five minutes?"

"Yes."

"That long?"

"Yes."

"Did you consider that I had fainted, or that I was in some kind of trouble?"

"No."

"May I ask why not?"

"I thought you were fooling around."

"You thought I was fooling around?"

"Yes."

Two fairly identical incidents such as those I have described should have led a reasonable person to *some* type of conclusion, I suppose. I *was* a bit perturbed at my wife's obliviousness but, as I've stated, it never occurred to me that she might actually wish me harm.

This was a simple oversight on her part. She had no reason to believe that my life had been in danger.

Could have happened to anybody, I thought. So, I stayed married to her.

Some years later, however, food poisoning struck me again, and this event unfolded very much like the last, except that my wife wasn't in the room when I passed out. She was, however, standing over me when I woke up. And I am quite sure I had interrupted her reading.

She spoke first.

"You're on the floor, you know..."

"Am I?"

"Yes."

"How did I get here?"

"I don't quite know."

"How long have I been here?"

"I'm not sure."

Even in my debilitated state, an old, familiar feeling of astonishment crept over me.

I tried to rise, found I couldn't, and lay back down on the

floor, where at least it appeared relatively safe.

My wife continued to tower over me, and it seemed she was waiting for me to make up my mind whether to expire or survive.

She sighed. "Wait here," she commanded somewhat impatiently, without meaning to be flippant, I am sure.

She returned with a towel soaked in cool water and pressed it against my brow. It felt good, and it was the first time in three near-death experiences – all in my wife's presence – that she had rendered any aid.

So I was encouraged. Overall, things were improving, and any suspicions I might have had seemed to be unfounded.

When I began this essay, I suggested that my wife doesn't suffer from poor judgment but that she merely has a personality that is different from mine. For instance, I'm inclined to leap before I look. I charge into action to fix this thing or that, usually without considering the consequences of any of my actions.

Andrea is one to sit back. Unlike her headstrong husband, she will wisely analyze and evaluate a situation carefully before she acts. And, she will continue to do so long after the time for action has passed. I've always thought we complement each other quite perfectly in this regard. So we've stayed married.

What I *really* think is that my wife simply doesn't recognize when I'm dying. While I'm pleased that she's typically spared the despair of watching me suffer, this alarms me. One day, God forbid, she may be called upon to resuscitate me, or pull me from a burning car, or carry out an emergency tracheotomy, or even dislodge a chicken bone stuck in my throat by performing the Heimlich maneuver in front of 200 dazed fellow-diners.

In sum, I don't know if I can count on my beloved to thwart my end if the need arises. But, hell, that's asking a lot, isn't it? After all, she's a wife, not Dr. Marcus Welby or Captain America. But, if I do succeed in killing myself off one day, I'm confident that Andrea's *description* of my sorry demise *after-the-fact* will be thorough and well-considered. Possibly, with an alternate ending.

All in all, I suppose it's just best to avoid doing foolish things and eating questionable food substances, like fried oysters from a roadside stand. I still pray that all wives everywhere will keep one ear and one eye on their husbands at all times. Hubby may be inclined to act imprudently or even recklessly on rare occasion, and one day he may need your assistance:

To keep him in existence.

It's Hard For A Father When His Daughters Are Mike Tyson And Mario Andretti

I WON'T BORE YOU UNDULY with gushing anecdotes about my daughters, Ariana and Stephanie. It's enough to say that they are audacious, brilliant, beautiful, trash-talking revolutionaries bent on their father's destruction.

Stephanie, my eldest, is something under five feet tall and a blue-eyed beauty. She is a dedicated dancer, having committed a full twenty hours a week for over a decade toward the endeavor. All things said, she's quick-witted, sharp-tongued, aggressive, low to the ground, lithe and powerful.

One fine evening, when she was about sixteen, I stood between this panther-like vixen and the front door in a narrow hallway in my home. She was on her way out for a night of partying of one kind or another (generically referred to by her as "hanging with my posse"). She was also more undressed than dressed for the occasion.

I'm always amazed how young women, who forget they will always be little girls in the eyes of their adoring fathers, seek to offend the delicate sensibilities of their rapidly aging Dads by finding ever-so-creative and innovative ways to thrust the confines of their small frames from between the various crevices of their clothing. This, no doubt, is meant to inspire other teenage girls, as well as to delight their male counterparts and troubadours who, at that age, are composed solely of muscle, bone, skin and testosterone in equal proportion.

While I was somewhat accustomed to this weekly spectacle – and generally powerless to affect the situation without risk to the peace of my household and the stability of my emotional state – I was riveted by what I considered a bust line so extreme as to compel Marilyn Chambers to blush and Gypsy Rose Lee to reach for a towel.

I had had enough. After all, was I not the head of the household? Doesn't a father have rights? Was I not the king of the forest, the breadwinner, the hot tamale, the big cheese?

Right. DAMN RIGHT. Enough was enough. I was putting my foot down.

I stood in that hallway with my hands on my hips, a living, breathing stereotype, with stereotypical phrases spewing from my mouth even before I could think them up.

"Just where do you think you're going dressed like that?" I demanded.

Stephanie shook her head back and forth in disbelief – spasmodically – as if she were shooing away an annoying insect.

"What did you say?" she asked.

She glared at me, then squinted her eyes and cocked her head like a German Shepherd that didn't understand its master's commands. She took the palms of her hands and smacked both of her ears as if to jog them back to a functioning state.

As memorable as that look of incredulity on her face was, I had seen it once before…It had been just a few months earlier. I was lying innocently in my bed on a lazy Saturday morning when my ever-so-charming and oh-so-persuasive offspring entered with her most adorable "Oh, Daddy, I love you so much!" face on.

She approached my bedside demurely and asked for a favor. I replied reflexively. "Of course, sweetheart, what do you need?"

She cooed that she "needed" $400 for "pictures." My mouth dropped open, my lips temporarily incapable of forming words, my eyes bulging from their sockets. I replied sweetly.

"What kind of pictures, darling?" She looked at me as if I were a dolt.

"What do you mean?" she snapped. "They're *pictures!*"

Of course they were. Was I deaf? Didn't I understand the English language? Limited by the parameters of my foolish question I could only foolishly repeat it, only using fewer words this time.

"Pictures?" I asked.

Like any good general, she altered her battle plan, no doubt in response to my formidable resistance and steadfast resolution. She sweetly ignored my naiveté, clasped her hands together in front of her and pursed her lips in a manner I found delightful.

"I'm making big pictures of all of my friends, putting them in frames and hanging them on the wall," she explained.

Stephanie was a popular girl and had many friends. Four hundred dollars' worth, apparently. Still, I was grateful for the clarification.

She took two steps forward and flashed her pearly whites so brilliantly that the hardest heart could only melt in response.

"Pleeeeeze?"

"No," I said. "You cannot have $400 for 'pictures.'"

That was when I saw that look on my daughter's face for the first time; a look of shock and awe even George Bush could never have imagined. A look one might project after seeing an alien, or a ghost, or Thor the Thunder God, or any other imaginary thing that could only exist *in theory* and NOT IN THE BEDROOM.

I confess that I was just as surprised as my dear daughter. I realized, as she undoubtedly did, that it was the first time in my life that I had said "no" to her. Of course, I immediately realized my error and, always quick to correct my mistakes, asked for my checkbook and disbursed the required sum.

But, that was *then*. *Now*, I'm going to take you just a few yards away, back to that hallway outside of my bedroom, where I faced my party-bound daughter and that look of incomprehension once more. My imposing presence filled the hall. This time I was strong.

Stephanie, always thinking of my health and well-being, advised me to move. I stood fast, both hands on my hips. I was resolute.

She told me to get out of her way immediately. I refused. I was

Father. But, I was more than that. I was *Man*.

She drove her right fist three inches deep into my solar plexus, putting her entire 102 pounds behind the blow. I retreated a full foot but somehow remained on my feet. I gasped, treasuring the oxygen remaining in my lungs, and knowing that little more was likely to enter there for some time. I wondered how long a person could live without breathing. More so, I wondered how long I could convince my daughter that I was unfazed by her puny blow.

I smiled, my body swaying gently from left to right. I shook my head back and forth. She about-faced, returned to her room in a huff, and slammed the door behind her. I seized a wall for support and doubled over, sucking in the stale air of the vestibule. I composed myself, retreated to the living room, and slumped into the couch.

I stayed there just long enough to stabilize my vital signs, and to witness Stephanie storm from her bedroom and out the front door wearing a conservative blue blouse buttoned up to her chin.

While I've never been struck by Mike Tyson, the blow I received from my daughter that day was harder than any I have taken from any man. But my youngest daughter, Ariana, topped her sister just a few months later…

We were in Ocean City, Maryland, on a family vacation, and at a local amusement park, where you could ride high-speed go-carts around a variety of complex, graded tracks. These things went forty miles an hour, and I approached the idea of a fourteen-year-old operating one with hesitation. Hell, I approached the idea of *me* driving one of these contraptions with hesitation as I watched them whiz around the surrounding tracks.

Ariana complements her sister nicely. She is brilliant and mature beyond her years, terribly cute, and charming when she wants to be. She's articulate and analytical as well, and prefers to form her arguments from facts obtained from careful research.

Which, invariably, lead to her own unavoidable conclusions.

But, at that age, she was still much *calmer* than her sister, and she listened. I would simply instruct her to drive slowly and follow me, and she would comply. I would watch out for her. After all, I was practically a professional driver.

I wasn't, of course, but I *had* worked as a cab driver for a year or two at college. I *had* shuttled cars long distance for Avis. Hell, I was a *New York* driver, for Pete's sake and let's not forget about that 450 horsepower Camaro I drove as a kid. Yeah.

Yeah. I could do this.

We climbed aboard three go-carts as my devil-may-care bride looked on.

Andrea is typically content to play the part of the *surviving* spouse. She prefers to be the one called upon to describe the accident to police, rather than assume the role of her unfortunate better half, who is selected to perish in the fiery crash.

A large, overhead traffic light, suspended by a wire across the track turned green. Some bearded carny on a ladder waved a tattered flag, and we took off. I immediately realized how powerful *go-things* are. They're low to the ground and have a wide wheelbase, but I felt as if I were going to tip end over end at any moment.

My two daughters simultaneously pealed the wheels of their respective vehicles and launched themselves from the starting gate. In what seemed an instant, they passed me by as little more than blurs and disappeared around the bend in the track.

I took the only rational course of action available to me: I pushed my foot down hard on the accelerator pedal and followed.

I was amazed at the sheer recklessness of my children. I was also amazed at how *jealous* I was that their driving abilities so far exceeded mine. I continued to advance, my heartbeat rising in perfect unison with the speed of the vehicle. I managed to attain a cruising speed of 29 mph, which to me had all the feel of 129. I found myself alone on the track with no other vehicles in sight.

Maybe that was why I was so surprised by what happened next. Because, the next moment something massive careened into me, something traveling at light speed, something cosmic, like a bolt of lightning, something that wakes you from whatever reverie you're in. Visions of flaming cars in the Daytona 500 came to my mind, along with images of stretchers and men in white caps with fire extinguishers and people standing in the stands with their hands over their mouths.

I gasped and struggled to maintain control of the vehicle; the entire left side of my body was stinging in pain. A go-cart whizzed by, wildly fish-tailing once, twice, then three times; then the driver somehow gained control. It finally shuddered its way to a stop. Black tire tracks snaked their way across the final 100 feet of roadway and the acrid smell of burnt rubber hung in the air. I pulled up to the right of the miniature race car, shaken and bruised, and looked to my left.

"Sorry, Daddy," Ariana cheerfully exclaimed, as she exited her vehicle.

She popped out of it like a piece of white bread from a toaster and joined her sister. They laughed wildly and took off, hand in hand, to the next ride, and surely their next brush with their father's death.

I slowly dragged my aching body from the deep pit of the little car and grabbed a metal guardrail for support with a shaky hand. My wife looked on with a look of both amusement and concern. She was hardly surprised, as I was frequently injured by my family, their pets, and other instrumentalities within their collective control.

I've never raced with Mario Andretti or his progeny and don't expect to. And, while I've been in several car accidents, some of a serious nature, no vehicle has hit me as hard or injured me as severely as the one powered by my youngest angel that day.

The Night Of A Thousand Jews (or How I Met My Wife)

EVERY MARRIED COUPLE has a story like this, don't we? Someone always asks to hear it, and someone always blushes, smiles coyly, pretends to resist, and then complies. Once the storyteller begins to relate the tale, a solemn duty falls to all those lost souls whose misfortune it is to be standing within earshot of the storytelling. They must listen closely and politely, smile often, sigh intermittently and, every now and then, gaze at their partners – male or female – and beam a gloriously sweet smile, as if to inquire why *he-she* hadn't done that, too.

Anyway, this is a story with a sweet kind of magic to it. While seasoned with a dash of self-serving debauchery it is, nevertheless, quite true.

I was in my early thirties and still single. My father was in his mid-sixties. It was the late eighties. It was a time when father and son thought of the future as if of one mind. When the son, with nothing but his father's fine example before him, contemplated his duty to perpetuate the family name and bloodline, settle down, build a family and construct a happy life.

With grandchildren, of course. Several, if possible. Well, those were the times, I suppose. But I can tell you that at that time this son had no intention of settling down. I considered my future to be my next weekend at the bars, and I gave not one instant's attention to thoughts of bloodline, pedigree or posterity.

Notwithstanding, one fine Saturday afternoon my father cornered my brother and me in the family room of his home, a knotted pine-paneled cave with a built-in bar and an octagonal poker table which doubled as a dinner table. He beamed as he displayed a two-by-four inch ad he had cut from a newspaper. The headline of the ad took up half of it. It read, in boldface type, as follows:

ONE THOUSAND

Jewish Singles

The advertisement promised this bounty at a weekend event to take place in two weeks at the Pines Hotel in upstate New York.

My father couldn't have been more pleased. He was more than happy to pay for our weekend, he said, on the oft chance that one of us (or praise be to God, if it were possible, *both* of us) would come home with the Jewish princess of our choice hanging limply from our arm.

I had no desire to be at a mountain retreat for three whole days and had little interest in Jewish women, *per se*. However, I also had to admit that the sheer potential *number* of them corralled together at one location *was* intriguing. That being said, I wasn't buying it.

My brother – not a lawyer yet, but well on his way – began negotiating. By the end, we had obtained the promise of a luxury hotel room and additional spending money to fund our activities. So, somewhat in a daze, we found ourselves up in the Catskill Mountains some time later.

It should come as no surprise to any of you that I found myself sauced in the rather hectic hotel bar at 2 a.m., just a few hours after we arrived, and I was pleased to discover that alcohol flowed just as freely at high altitudes as at sea level. These days, of course, I limit my drinking: first, because I consider myself foolish enough when I'm sober, and second, because I become happy if I don't. As most married Jewish men are fully aware, this is an emotional state that is strictly forbidden. But *then*, I was *permitted* to be happy, and I thought nothing of taking down four or five drinks if I wasn't getting into a car.

There were a couple of memorable things about that evening. Well, they were memorable for *me*, and you're going to hear about them, too, because it's the end of the book and you're not going to stop reading now.

A bunch of guys had crowded around me for some reason, as if I were the only cool guy in the room. I certainly *felt* like the only cool guy, because *these* guys were a little too *un-cool* for me. In any event, one of them pointed out a pretty girl across the room who he knew from high school.

I got an idea. I asked him to tell me everything he remembered about her, which was quite a lot. I absorbed what I could, then turned to the other fellows and told them to position themselves discretely around the girl, but within earshot, and wait for the show. They giggled and retreated to their places.

I took a wide berth and approached the girl from the rear.

I hope that came out right.

In any event, her name was Sharon. I walked right by her then stopped in my tracks and seized my head in both hands as if I were in great pain. I peeked over my shoulder at her, wincing.

I don't remember a single detail about her life now, or the exact words of any sentence I uttered to her. But I certainly remember the tone and tenor of our conversation. It went something like this:

"You're Sharon, right?"

"Yes. Do I know you?"

"No, I don't think so. But, you went to Roosevelt High, right?"

"Yes! How do you know me?"

"I don't. It's just...well...it's just that I have a bit of a psychic sense. There are certain people that for some reason are connected to me. I get these *flashes*, sometimes."

I grabbed my head again and shuddered. She took a few steps closer and placed a hand on my arm.

"Are you OK?" she asked, genuinely concerned.

I ignored her question. "You had that teacher, Mr. Sonorio, right?" I asked through painfully squinted eyes.

"And, you had a friend...a good friend, with black hair, named Dora."

"That's right!" she exclaimed, quite delighted. "You're amazing!"

I had little reason to correct her, particularly when she was being so correct. I won't go on with any further description of this snapshot because it really gets stupid from here. Suffice it to say that I had my laugh and began to leave the bar at around 2:30 in the morning.

Just before I did, I pointed out to my newfound colleagues – who were terribly impressed by my recent performance – that the forty-year-old hottie by the bar really *was* looking for someone to talk to, and if they wanted me to prove it, that I would. I struck up a nice conversation with her, too, until my bar buddies took that as a sign that the ice had been broken, found their courage, and determined that it was safe for the five of them to move in on her simultaneously.

As I said, I left. But as I did, I noticed a table just to the left of the exit. On that table was a blonde, fast asleep, head down, as if she were a little girl taking a nap at her desk at nursery school. As I had been on a roll the entire evening, I figured I'd conclude the night with one final guffaw.

I tapped the dreamer on the shoulder. She awoke in a moderate stupor and looked up at me, dazed and confused, as the old record says. I cordially reminded her that she was in a hotel, that there were plenty of beds right up the stairs and that perhaps she might wish to avail herself of the hotel's generous amenities.

Thoroughly pleased with my obnoxiousness, I withdrew to my luxury suite. Ten minutes later, I was asleep.

I awoke abruptly at 9:45 the following morning; abruptly because my brother was punching me in the shoulder and yelling at me.

He was *roaring* at me, actually, and trying to tell me that they stopped serving breakfast in 15 minutes and that we had to get downstairs because he had to eat. He has this blood sugar thing, you see, and when Matt gets like this, you don't want to get between him and his English muffin. I got up, and the room spun around me, instantly reminding me of the marvelous time I had the night before. Matthew and I threw on clothes, donned pairs of dark-black sunglasses that the hotel provided all its guests for the weekend, and rushed downstairs.

What greeted us there was what had been advertised. There were at least a thousand people in a dining room the size of a football field. Each and every one of them was wearing their standard-issue sunglasses. All of them, no doubt, were also recovering from the prior night's festivities.

Scores of large round tables accommodated about ten guests each, and they seemed to stretch the entire length of the Northern Hemisphere, disappearing over a false horizon before us that seemed a hundred miles away. We arrived just moments before breakfast terminated, and every seat in the house appeared occupied.

We walked through the seemingly endless rows of tables, each one crammed with dazed twenty and thirty-somethings with lens-shuttered eyes, busily munching away. If I'd been just a bit more dazed than I was, I would've thought we'd stumbled upon a field of carcasses with thousands of hungry flies greedily feeding off of them. Matt was getting quite agitated because he was really getting *whacked* by his fluctuating glucose levels, and because there didn't appear to be an empty seat (or empty mouth, for that matter) in the entire joint.

After hiking for what seemed days, we found two contiguous, vacant seats at a table that was about three-quarters deep into the expansive dining area. We sat down. Matt began to adjust his silverware greedily in anticipation of his meal, although I had serious doubts if he cared whether he was going to feast on bacon and eggs or road kill.

Still, I wasn't comfortable. I sat stiffly and with straightened back at full attention at the table. This spot wasn't "right." I have no rational explanation for why this strange feeling descended upon me, but it did. For some reason, I didn't want to sit there. I turned to my brother.

"I don't want to sit here," I said.

"What?" he asked, rather predictably.

"I don't want to sit here," I repeated.

"Why?" was his sole query, his uncontrollable hunger compelling him to reserve his mouth for more vital duties by limiting his vocabulary to efficient, one-word responses.

"I just don't want to sit here," I repeated.

I should have felt stupid, but I didn't. Hey, I was the older brother. One of the advantages of being an older brother is that you can make any ridiculous statement to your sibling. Furthermore, you can properly anticipate that while its rationale may very well escape you, its meaning should be perfectly clear to him.

"There are no more seats!" my brother pleaded with bulging eyes that conveyed both incredulity and exasperation, and a less-than-subtle fear of impending hospitalization.

"Come on," I said, rising from my seat, disgusted by his whining and amazed by his foolishness. I confidently strode away in the direction we had been heading just moments before.

I truly don't know what I was thinking at the time. In fact, I don't think I was thinking at all. It wasn't exactly a "hunch" or a "feeling" I was acting upon; it was something else. It was more like a reaction, like when the poles of two magnets touch and repulse each other. Or when they're pulled to each other.

My confident stride soon deteriorated to an uncertain meander as I realized that the dining hall terminated just a dozen or so yards ahead. Still, I walked on, my false bravado ebbing with every step. As fate would have it, as they say, there were two seats remaining at a table at the far end of the space.

We approached timidly, hesitant for any sign that someone might be returning. We paused briefly behind our proposed seating, our eyes darting surreptitiously to the left, then to the right, then focusing on the communal platters of cheese, fruit, muffins, and pastries already on the table.

We sat down, my brother clearly relieved. We dug in greedily, both of us reaching for foodstuffs with both hands. We must have gorged ourselves for fifteen minutes before we took our eyes from our plates. Eventually, though, I looked up.

Across the table was a blonde-haired woman about my age, with dark sunglasses on her brow. I paused in dim recognition. She looked at me and smiled. She had been the recipient of my closing suavity at the hotel bar the night before. We struck up a conversation and, after breakfast, I asked if she would like to sit and chat in the hotel lobby for a while. She agreed.

I knew I was going to marry her about fifteen minutes into that conversation, and there wasn't much thought involved with that conviction, either. That, too, was just a reaction.

Think magnets. Sigh.

Presently, a Whitney Houston song began to play gently through the speakers located throughout the lobby. I slowly (and, quite dramatically, as I recall) rose to my feet. My eyes twinkled with both mischief and affection. At that moment, I was *totally* Charles Boyer. I touched her hand and asked her to dance. She smiled at my foolish gallantry and accepted. As we did, I whispered these words into her ear...

"...remember this song. One day, it might be important."

At our wedding reception, two and one-half years later, our first dance as a married couple was to the sound of that Whitney Houston melody.

I cannot pretend to explain how or why some things work out as they do. There's no doubt we have a say in the matter, and that our decisions help to form our ultimate realities.

But, I have come to believe that our lives are the result of any combination of things. Perhaps it is that time and chance doth happeneth to us all, as the Great Scribe said, and that random forces combine to weave the fabric of our experiences. Maybe it is that certain people are connected to each other, linked together somehow by an invisible thread. Maybe there is such a thing as fate, or destiny, or perchance there is a divine hand that intervenes to point people in a direction that is proper and good.

Or as my dear wife might say, maybe I just got lucky.

The End

Other Books by David I. Aboulafia:

MORE SNAPSHOTS? From My Uneventful Life
Roundfire Books
ISBN:

Visions Through a Glass, Darkly
Cosmic Egg Books
ISBN: 978-1-78535-022-1 (2016)

Correspondence to the Author can be Addressed to:

228 East 45th Street, Suite 1700
New York, NY 10017

Roundfire

FICTION

Put simply, we publish great stories. Whether it's literary or popular, a gentle tale or a pulsating thriller, the connecting theme in all Roundfire fiction titles is that once you pick them up you won't want to put them down.
If you have enjoyed this book, why not tell other readers by posting a review on your preferred book site. Recent bestsellers from Roundfire are:

The Bookseller's Sonnets
Andi Rosenthal

The Bookseller's Sonnets intertwines three love stories with a tale of religious identity and mystery spanning five hundred years and three countries.
Paperback: 978-1-84694-342-3 ebook: 978-184694-626-4

Birds of the Nile
An Egyptian Adventure
N.E. David

Ex-diplomat Michael Blake wanted a quiet birding trip up the Nile – he wasn't expecting a revolution.
Paperback: 978-1-78279-158-4 ebook: 978-1-78279-157-7

Blood Profit$
The Lithium Conspiracy
J. Victor Tomaszek, James N. Patrick, Sr.

The blood of the many for the profits of the few... *Blood Profit$*
will take you into the cigar-smoke-filled room where American
policy and laws are really made.
Paperback: 978-1-78279-483-7 ebook: 978-1-78279-277-2

The Burden
A Family Saga
N.E. David

Frank will do anything to keep his mother and father apart. But
he's carrying baggage – and it might just weigh him down ...
Paperback: 978-1-78279-936-8 ebook: 978-1-78279-937-5

The Cause
Roderick Vincent

The second American Revolution will be a fire lit from an
internal spark.
Paperback: 978-1-78279-763-0 ebook: 978-1-78279-762-3

Don't Drink and Fly
The Story of Bernice O'Hanlon: Part One
Cathie Devitt

Bernice is a witch living in Glasgow. She loses her way in her
life and wanders off the beaten track looking for the garden of
enlightenment.
Paperback: 978-1-78279-016-7 ebook: 978-1-78279-015-0

Gag
Melissa Unger

One rainy afternoon in a Brooklyn diner, Peter Howland
punctures an egg with his fork. Repulsed, Peter pushes the plate
away and never eats again.
Paperback: 978-1-78279-564-3 ebook: 978-1-78279-563-6

The Master Yeshua
The Undiscovered Gospel of Joseph
Joyce Luck

Jesus is not who you think he is. The year is 75 CE. Joseph ben
Jude is frail and ailing, but he has a prophecy to fulfil …
Paperback: 978-1-78279-974-0 ebook: 978-1-78279-975-7

On the Far Side, There's a Boy
Paula Coston

Martine Haslett, a thirty-something 1980s woman, plays hard on
the fringes of the London drag club scene until one night which
prompts her to sign up to a charity. She writes to a young Sri
Lankan boy, with consequences far and long.
Paperback: 978-1-78279-574-2 ebook: 978-1-78279-573-5

Tuareg
Alberto Vazquez-Figueroa

With over 5 million copies sold worldwide, *Tuareg* is a
classic adventure story from best-selling author
Alberto Vazquez-Figueroa, about honour, revenge and a
clash of cultures.
Paperback: 978-1-84694-192-4

Readers of ebooks can buy or view any of these bestsellers by clicking on the live link in the title. Most titles are published in paperback and as an ebook. Paperbacks are available in traditional bookshops. Both print and ebook formats are available online.

Find more titles and sign up to our readers' newsletter at http://www.johnhuntpublishing.com/fiction

Follow us on Facebook at
https://www.facebook.com/JHPfiction
and Twitter at https://twitter.com/JHPFiction